The

Max Hennessy was the pen-name of John Harris. He had a wide variety of jobs from sailor to cartoonist and became a highly inventive, versatile writer. In addition to crime fiction, Hennessy was a master of the war novel and drew heavily on his experiences in both the navy and air force, serving in the Second World War. His novels reflect the reality of war mixed with a heavy dose of conflict and adventure.

Also by Max Hennessy

The Martin Falconer Thrillers

The Fledglings
The Professionals
The Victors
The Interceptors
The Revolutionaries

The RAF Trilogy

The Bright Blue Sky
The Challenging Heights
Once More the Hawks

The Captain Kelly Maguire Trilogy

The Lion at Sea
The Dangerous Years
Back to Battle

The Flying Ace Thrillers

The Mustering of the Hawks
The Mercenaries
The Courtney Entry

The
INTERCEPTORS

JOHN HARRIS WRITING AS
MAX HENNESSY

⑩CANELO

First published in the United Kingdom in 1977 by The Anchor Press Ltd

This edition published in the United Kingdom in 2022 by

Canelo
Unit 9, 5th Floor
Cargo Works, 1-2 Hatfields
London, SE1 9PG
United Kingdom

A CIP catalogue record for this book is available from the British Library.

Print ISBN 978 1 80032 846 4
Ebook ISBN 978 1 80032 081 9

Look for more great books at www.canelo.co

Printed and bound in Great Britain by Clays Ltd, Elcograf S.p.A.

I

Chapter 1

For winter the sky was magnificent.

There was a good deal of stratocumulus around four thousand feet and the sun was flaring through a red western mist, the circle of the horizon reflected in its glow. Although higher up to the east there was another thin line of advancing cloud, the afternoon still had a bright alert look about it and the aeroplane felt safe under my hands.

Like every SE5 I'd ever handled it was a pleasure to control. It was roomy, with a comfortable cushioned seat, and I was well protected from the slipstream behind the padded rim of the fuselage. The engine was quiet compared with a Camel, an in-line job with long exhausts, and there was none of the nauseating smell of castor oil that came from the exhausts of rotary engines and affected a pilot's inside.

I

As I banked her and put her into a climb, to level off at ten thousand feet, I could see a vast plain of white cloud below me, sparkling in the sun, alabaster castles and snowy rainbowed valleys, with here and there gaps through which I could see darker shadows of the earth. The light was brilliant and seemed to come from every direction at once so that the immensity of the sky was a crystal clear bowl of blue, where the sun was brighter than normal people on their own two feet ever saw it. With only the drumming, sighing and creaking of the aeroplane and the smell of dope and the wind for company, I felt my spirit surge with elation.

When they'd chopped me out of the wreck of that Camel in Eastern France a few days before the Armistice I'd thought then – as they had – that I'd never fly again. But we were all wrong. There was more solid bone in my skull than any of us imagined and when they'd finished taking out the splinters the German bullet had lifted under my scalp, I was as right as rain again and within a few days of the Armistice was looking for food and itching to get out of bed. And now here I was, early in 1919, watching the fabric above the spars rippling with the passage of air over them and the sparkle of light through the propeller, and feeling I was one of God's chosen few.

The thought that I was sitting on a wicker-work seat a mile above the earth suspended only by the pull of a motor and the spread of the wings entranced me as it always did and, as I looked down at the glimpses of blue-tinted earth below, dazzled by the light of the sky, I was conscious of a sense of superiority over all other human beings.

As I dropped the machine towards the aero-drome I decided that I wanted to go on flying for ever and I wondered what Charley would say. Charley was a girl of strong views, but she was also a girl with a marked show of humour and a great deal of common-sense, and I decided that she'd not stand in my way.

I put the aeroplane down in a perfect three-pointer, deciding for the thousandth time that there was no sweeter feeling in the world than a good landing. I'd often been told that anyone could get an aeroplane off the ground and fly it but that it took a bit more than guesswork to put it down again, and it was true. Billy Bishop, who'd been one of the greatest fliers on the Western Front, always used to claim that he didn't land, he arrived, and I'd been guilty of a few 'arrivals' in my own career, but this time I touched down as gently as thistledown, feeling blessed among men.

There was a message waiting for me at the hangar as I climbed from the cockpit. 'Mr Falconer,' the flight-sergeant said, 'you've to telephone the mess.'

'It's a note that was left, sir,' the steward told me when I contacted him. 'It just says "Cavalry Club, 6 p.m. Ludo". Does it mean anything, sir?'

'Not at the moment,' I admitted. 'But I expect it will eventually.'

It sounded cryptic but Ludo Sykes, who was Charley's cousin, was never one to waste words, and I wondered what he was up to this time, because I'd thought for a long time that, if the stuffed shirts of the Navy didn't manage to destroy the infant Royal Air Force, as they seemed to be trying very hard to do now that the war was over, he was going to go a long way. I'd known him since 1915 when I was a boy not long out of school and he was a young captain recently out of a crack Hussar regiment trying to encourage the Royal Flying Corps to come up to cavalry standards of elegance, casual indifference and good manners. He was now a lieutenant-colonel.

I'd managed to end the war as a major, but they'd insisted when the guns stopped that, since I was staying in the Air Force, I must drop a rank. I hadn't had it long and I was still a bit young to throw my weight about, it seemed, and it was rather embarrassing in peacetime having majors around who were still officially minors.

I got a lift into London and found Sykes sitting in a deep armchair under a painting of the Marquess of Anglesey at Waterloo. He ordered me a drink and leaned forward to tap the medal ribbons under my wings. 'Got quite a lot of those now, young Brat,' he said.

I tapped his in return. 'Yours are prettier,' I said. 'And carry more weight.'

He smiled at me, full of the sort of lazy charm that made lesser mortals like me melt in front of him. 'Ever thought what you're going to do with 'em now the war's over?' he asked.

'You once said I should stay in the Air Force,' I pointed out. 'I decided to.'

'Well, Trenchard always had his eye on you. Ever since that day you told him to go to hell.'

'I wasn't myself at the time,' I said. 'I'd just demolished about a dozen poplar trees with a Camel and he wanted to know if I was all right.'

'Concerned, shouldn't wonder. That baby face of yours.'

'Perhaps I'd better grow a moustache again.'

'Shouldn't bother. Last one looked like a bit of fluff on your upper lip.' Sykes shifted in his chair and changed the subject. 'Know anything about Russia?' he asked.

I wondered what was coming. 'Well, it's big,' I said. 'And cold. And they ride in sledges, wear beards and have names that end in "ski".'

'That all?'

I stared at him. 'What's behind all this?' I asked.

Sykes smiled – that aloof cavalry smile of his that seemed to suggest the world was a bit of a bore and that the war had been a rather unseemly affair that had needed cavalry manners to give it a bit of tone. It didn't pay to take too much notice of it, because Coe Ludovic Bartelott-Dyveton-Sykes was a lot sharper than he pretended to be – certainly sharp enough to whip my girlfriend from under my nose in 1917 and marry her when I wasn't looking.

'What's behind it?' he said. 'All sorts of things. Come on—' he leaned forward '—you know more about Russia than that it's big and cold and they have names ending in "ski".'

'Well, they had a Tsar, but they haven't any more.'

'Getting warmer.'

'They shot him, didn't they?'

'Go on. Why?'

'Because they had a revolution.'

'Full marks. Ten for effort. That's why I asked. Now – how are you finding peace?'

I knew there was *something* in the wind. Sykes was never arch and clever without good reason, and I played along with him.

'Bit bored,' I said. 'Especially now that they've finished taking pieces of bone out of my head and pronounced me fit again.'

'Affect your flying?'

I gave him a sideways look. 'I went to Brooklands this morning,' I said. 'They let me take up an SE. I threw it all round the sky. It didn't seem to do me much harm.'

'Good.' Sykes was still smiling. He leaned back again. 'Saw Munro t'other day.'

Jock Munro had done two and a half tours with me in France between 1917 and the end of the war and like Ludo seemed to be part of my background.

'Is he in London?' I asked. 'I always thought the only thing he wanted was to marry that girl, Barbara Hatherley, and to go back to Aberdeen.'

'Changed his mind, shouldn't wonder. Saw him at the Air Ministry.'

'How is he?'

'Still hobbling about. Fixed him up with some flying. Seemed to do him good. Might do you good, too.'

I sat up and stared straight at him. '"Russia",' I said. '"Munro". "How's your flying?" Come on, Ludo. Spit it out. What's on?'

He grinned. 'Going to Russia, old boy.'

'Who is?'

'I am. So's Munro.'

'And you're wondering if I'd like to come, too?'

'Would you?'

'What's Charley going to say?' I asked. 'She's been pretty patient.'

Sykes shrugged. 'Over to a meal the other night,' he said. 'Primed her a little. Told her it would be good for your career and all that. Seemed to suspect you'd be going, anyway. Think you might?'

'Yes,' I admitted. 'I think I might. Tell me some more.'

He settled back and began to explain. 'Well,' he said, 'when the Bolsheviks had their revolution in 1917 and took Russia out of the war we all thought that was that. But it wasn't. The Treaty of Brest-Litovsk allowed the Germans to pour into Finland, Lithuania and the Ukraine, outwardly to help the Bolshevik Russian government but in fact to snatch as much food as possible to minimize the Allied blockade of Germany and grab all of the stores at Archangel, Murmansk and Vladivostok that we'd sent to Russia while they were still in the war.'

I waited patiently. Sykes had his own way of going about things, and he'd obviously decided a little background music was in order.

'No point in going into all the details,' he went on. 'About how the Czechs in Russia formed an army to fight Austria, the oppressor of their homeland, and how, after the revolution when it was decided to send them home, they quarrelled with the Bolsheviks and seized the Trans-Siberian railway. You'll not know much about that. You were still a schoolboy at the time.'

'I could read the newspapers,' I said. 'I'd learned my ABC.'

He smiled. 'Anyway, the success of the Czechs set off several other counter-revolutions and their leaders were given courage by the presence of British and French troops which had been landed to guard those stores of ours against the Germans. Then Allied military missions began to arrive – to train troops and so on. You still with me?'

'Sitting right in your lap.'

'Well, because everyone at this end of Europe had begun to get the wind up that Bolshevism would spread right across the Continent – after all, it brought down the German Emperor – a few people like Clemenceau, Winston Churchill and one or two more decided it might be a good idea to help the counter-revolutionaries to give Russia a government that might be more acceptable to the rest of the world. They think now that they'll succeed, because the counter-revolutionary armies – called White so as to be opposite to Red, I suppose – hope to reach Moscow and Petrograd simultaneously from east, north-west and south.'

'Nothing any army ever did,' I said, 'ever managed to be simultaneous. If they manage it, it'll be sheer luck.'

He smiled. 'Well, there *is* that. All the same, a chap called Kolchak, in Siberia, backed by British, American and Japanese forces, is organizing a mass advance across the Volga. Another chap called Yudenich is striking down from Estonia, while in the south where I'm going, there's a chap called Denikin who's heading north, his left wing making for Kiev and his right – under a chap called Wrangel – driving along the Volga. They think they'll reach Moscow by Christmas.'

'So?'

He gestured languidly. 'So now, in addition to sending instructors, which is all that they've been sending so far, the British government's decided a little help from intrepid birdmen like you and me might possibly come in handy. Raymond Collishaw – remember him? Quite a flyer; sixty-odd Huns, wasn't it? – he's got two flights of bombers and one of Camels. I've got the same. Aeroplanes aren't all that new, of course, but they ought to be all right, and officially we shall be the only operational units in Russia. Keeping tabs on the enemy's movements, you might say, but I think it'll end up as more than that – what you might call flying Cossacks, or government-hired gladiators.'

'Defenders of law and order,' I said. 'Champions of the weak and oppressed.'

He grinned. 'Guerillas,' he ended. 'Mercenaries. Hired janizaries, allies, co-operators, interceptors, nosy parkers, bashi-bazouks. Take your pick.'

We sat back and smiled at each other.

'And you want me to go with you?' I said.

'I shall mostly be polishing the seat of a chair in the office and liaising with the Russians or British HQ, so I want someone good to run the flights for me. I've got two good chaps for the DH9s, and I can't think of anybody better than you for the Camels. You'll get back your old rank and I've got some good people for you – all Camel experts. Munro, for instance; Jasper, from 66 Squadron; Stagg, from 28; Hardinge, from 203. And a chap called Jimmy Slingsby, from 70, who looks even younger than you – though he isn't – and, if anything, is probably madder. He's reputed to have chased a hare across the field at Izel-le-Hameau at nought feet. What do you say?'

I grinned. 'Try and stop me,' I said.

I'd read about the revolution in Russia, of course, and having served in France until 1918 when the British Army had emerged as the only one that hadn't suffered political disintegration, I didn't have much time for mutinous soldiers who shot their officers in the back or for the sharp-witted gentlemen who'd deposed the Tsar. As a result, although I had a shrewd idea that the Tsar had been a bit indifferent both as a leader and as a monarch, to me the revolution wasn't a fight by oppressed workers to put right a great many wrongs, but a struggle by a lot of evil people to do away with the stable society to which I belonged.

Most other Englishmen of my background felt much the same. Perhaps none of us was very clever and perhaps we suffered from far too much idealism, but idealism was part of our generation and had sent men rushing to the recruiting offices in 1914 and led them to death on the knuckled hills of the Somme and in the swampy wastes of Passchendaele. Even after four years of war it hadn't died completely and, in a way, I felt a visit to Russia would not only strike a blow for law and order, but would also give me time to adjust to peace and do no harm to my career in the Air Force either.

Sykes was to leave within a week but, because I still had to be cleared by the doctors, I should be travelling separately. Since the idea of heading into the obscurity of Holy Russia on my own was rather a daunting prospect and since Munro was being delayed for the same reason I was, I decided I'd better look him up so we could arrange to travel together.

I found him at Cranwell and got the steward to page him. 'Captain *Hector Horatio* Munro,' I insisted. 'Not just "Munro". The lot.'

I waited by the bar, listening as the steward shouted in the ante-room doorway, and a few minutes later Munro appeared, hobbling furiously in like an angry spider. 'Wha' the hell—?' he began. Then he saw me.

'Brat Falconer!' he yelled. 'Ah wondered who it was shoutin' ma names aroond because they're a secret Ah'm always careful tae keep.'

His accent was as thick as ever but he looked a lot better than when I'd last seen him as he was dragged out of the wreckage of his machine not long before the end of the war, with his face carved up and the water the stretcher-bearers were pouring into his mouth running out through a hole in his chin and on to his chest. His bony Scots features were criss-crossed by the raw-looking scars of his crash but he seemed to have discarded one of the two sticks he had used to help him walk and was managing very well as far as I could see.

'I thought you were going back to Scotland,' I said. 'I always thought a star hung in the sky over Aberdeen.'

'Aye, well—' he paused '—mebbe Ah'm growin' older. There doesnae seem tae be the pull there used tae be and there isnae much flyin' up there. In the same way, there doesnae seem tae be the laughter.' He looked indignant. 'Nobody joins in when Ah play the piano these days.'

'It's a bit different since the war ended,' I agreed. 'People aren't so sentimental and they haven't time these days to go in for those bloodbaths of nostalgia we used to enjoy in France.' I smiled. 'Besides, they've probably realized at last what a rotten pianist you are.'

His indignation deepened and I hurried on before he could start arguing. 'I thought you were going to get married,' I said.

'Aye, well—' he paused and frowned. 'Her family emigrated, y'see, and they insisted on her gaein' wi' 'em. They want her to wait for a few months in case it was just a wartime romance. Ah think they're mebbe hopin' Ah'll fall apart at the seams if we leave it long enough, and that'll be that.' He grinned. 'Actually, Ah thought Ah might get the pill-rollers tae take me apart an' put me taegether again. It'd mebbe be easier.'

'They could use clockwork this time,' I said. 'I'd wind you up every twenty-four hours when I did my watch.'

He grinned. 'They could mebbe even arrange a pendulum. Then if ye saw me runnin' doon, all ye'd have tae do would be tae gie it a wee kick. How aboot yer noddle?'

'They took out a few lumps of iron.'

We stopped, staring at each other, both knowing I wasn't there simply to ask questions about Munro's health. I jumped in at the deep end.

'Ludo says you're going to Russia,' I said abruptly.

He smiled. 'Ah thought it'd kill the time a bit till they let Barbara off the hook, and Ah can mebbe earn a few bawbees intae the bargain. How aboot you? What are you up tae?'

'I'm going to Russia, too.'

His face lit up. 'Ye're no'?' Then his grin died again. 'But what aboot yon gel – Sykes' cousin – Charley – what's she got tae say aboot it?'

'Aye, well,' I said, mocking him gently, 'that's something I've still got to sort out.'

–

It turned out to be very different from what I'd expected.

Charley – Charlotte Margaret Caroline Bartelott-Dyveton-Sykes to give her full name – was certainly going to have *something* to say and I was a little nervous about facing her. She belonged to one of the oldest families in the country and when Sykes had pinched my girl and married her I'd consoled myself with Charley whom I'd met at the engagement party. She'd still been a giggler in those days but, with eighteen months' nursing, several of them in France, she'd grown up a lot since then and she left me in no doubt about her attitude.

'Ludo's doing, I suppose,' she said coolly. 'I heard he was off again and I thought he'd be after you. From the voice of doom you used when you telephoned, it wasn't hard to guess he'd got you.'

'Do you mind, Charley?'

She exploded. 'Of course I mind, you ass! After all the time I spent putting you together after the crash, you surely don't think I enjoy seeing you panting to bust yourself up all over again, do you?'

'Perhaps I won't bust myself up.'

'I bet you do,' she snorted. 'You and danger seem to go together. Twice I've done it. That time when you crashed in Yorkshire and again just before the Armistice. You'll end up as a little bent old man crippled with arthritis, with all your legs and arms in a sling. I think you're barmy. The last I heard, you weren't ever going to be fit for flying again.'

'Yes, well—' I sounded like Munro as I searched for the right words to reply '—I've discovered I am.'

'You've been up?'

'Once or twice.'

'Heaven preserve us!' Her eyes glowed with indignation. 'I'll be having a word with Cousin Ludo, you'll see. That man's cunning makes Machiavelli and the Borgia lot look like Charlie Chaplin.'

It seemed that her feelings were stronger than I'd expected and I surrendered without resistance.

'All right, Charley,' I said, trying to put the best face on it I could. 'If that's the way you feel, I won't go.'

She whirled. '*What?*'

'I said I won't go.'

'Just because *I* said you shouldn't?' Her expression was a little awed.

'Yes.'

Her fierce expression melted and she leaned forward and gave me an unexpected peck on the cheek. 'Thank you for that, Martin,' she said quietly. 'I believe you, too, as it happens. But you'd eat your heart out, wouldn't you?'

I tried to look as if I wouldn't but I obviously didn't make a very good job of it. She frowned.

'Now you've made *me* feel rotten,' she said. 'I knew when I first met you that you were sold on flying so I can't ask you to give it all up and become a grocer or something.'

'I could try.'

'No! You've got to do what you want to do and, in any case, when I'm in my dotage, it'll be nice to look at you and think how clever you were to become a general.'

'Now *you're* talking silly.'

'Don't kid yourself. You'll end up covered with stars, sashes, ribbons, and all that rot.'

'Full of martial glory and handsome as the devil?' I said.

She looked at me sideways. 'People who want to stay *that* handsome shouldn't fly aeroplanes into the cold hard ground.' She gave me one of those electric grins of hers that, like Sykes's, could charm the ducks off the water. 'I think you're smashing, Martin,' she said. 'Honest.' Her expression slipped a little. 'Only don't expect cries of wild delight, will you, because I'll miss you like the very dickens. However—' she cheered up again, mercurial as ever '—as it happens, between you and me and the gatepost, the parents have been dropping strong hints that, as you're still not yet officially an adult and I'm still practically a babe in arms, we ought not to rush things. And now that the war's over and you're not going to get killed, perhaps they're right. In any case, I have a feeling you've got a lot of travelling to do before you settle down. Will it take long?'

'Lord knows. What if it does?'

She gave me that superior smile of hers that made me feel like a little boy. 'I'll wait, of course. There's just one thing.'

I was so grateful to her for making it so easy, I'd have promised her anything. 'What?'

'Just keep away from all those countesses and baronesses and things. Ludo says Russia's full of 'em.'

Chapter 2

It wasn't until we reached sub-tropical Batum on the Black Sea that it dawned on me that Charley had made no mention of any fighting and I had a sudden suspicion that Sykes had probably skated over that part of it so that she was under the impression I was going out like so many others merely as an instructor.

We had travelled via Le Havre, Modane, Turin and Athens, and in Athens we met our first Russian refugees. They all seemed to be wealthy and, because they'd been wise enough to leave Russia in good time, they didn't appear to be suffering much from being dispossessed by the revolution. From them we learned something of the background of the White armies we were going to join.

The first military resistance to the revolution, it seemed, had been started by a General Kornilov, who'd been put in command of the mutinous garrison at Petrograd in 1917 but had resigned because he wasn't allowed to restore discipline. Fleeing across Russia to the Don, he'd been joined by a General Alexeiev, a former commander-in-chief, and had built a new army to combat both the Germans and the Bolsheviks. Both Kornilov and Alexeiev were dead now, Kornilov of wounds, Alexeiev of typhus, but they'd wrought a miracle between them, and Cossacks from the Don, the Kuban and the Terek were rallying in hundreds to the White cause. There'd been setbacks, of course, but the Bolshevik southward movement had finally lost its momentum and eventually been pushed back; and, with Novorossiisk and Sebastopol as seaports, and Ekaterinodar, the city named for Catherine the Great, just to the north as a base, the White armies were increasing in size and, now, with British and French intervention, were hoping to drive the Bolsheviks back to Moscow.

There were a lot of British officers at Batum waiting to join the British Mission. Some of them had been prisoners of the Germans and were hoping to catch up on some of the promotion they'd missed while in prisoner-of-war camps; and some were men who'd spent most of the war in

France doing very well, thank you, in back areas, and clearly intended to do the same again in Russia. There was a lot of indifference and, because one or two had died in the typhus epidemics which seemed to sweep Batum from time to time, a lot of them clearly had no intention of getting too involved with the Russians – 'That lot,' as they called them.

Batum was shrouded in mist all the time we were there, with the oil smell from the refineries heavy on the still air. We just had enough time to see as much of it as we wanted – which wasn't very much – and then we were embarked for Novorossiisk. The spring thaw was just starting when we arrived, and the town, grey beneath the onion-shaped domes of the churches, seemed to consist entirely of mud. In places it was ankle-deep, and the boards and stones which had been laid down for pedestrians to cross the roads were already disappearing from sight underneath it. It seemed to be everywhere, on the walls, on the wheels of vehicles, on boots and clothes, hampering the traffic and slowing down everything that went on. The town seemed to wallow in it, and there was a constant procession of people struggling to the wooden sidewalks as their horses or their cars became bogged down axle-deep.

Houses and rooms were at a premium. With all the refugees from the north crowding into the place as well as the troops that were gathering there as reinforcements for the armies to the north, rooms and houses had been let and sub-let, and sub-let again, until no one knew who was actually in residence and it was virtually impossible to find somewhere to sleep.

The streets were full of penniless refugees and the place was a hotbed of crime, with the White Army's printed money practically valueless. There was the same motley assortment of races there'd been in Batum – Russian soldiers in British khaki, ex-Tsarist officers in grey greatcoats lined in scarlet silk with epaulettes like planks on their shoulders, foreign businessmen newly arrived after the war in Europe to make the first doubtful steps into the chaos the revolution had caused, Levantine merchants, Cossacks in fur caps and strung about with weapons, dubious-looking women, Jews in ancient black coats and hats, villainous-looking Balkan adventurers, Turks, speculators, militia, and

German and Austrian prisoners of war awaiting repatriation.

Many of the Russians had been wealthy before the revolution but they were now having to live in appalling conditions, crowded into tiny rooms cluttered with their belongings and smelling of the creosote they used to try to discourage the wild life. Everywhere in South Russia seemed to be crowded and it wasn't hard to pick up any disease you could mention, from smallpox to diphtheria or typhus to cholera. Though the Bolsheviks were a long way to the north everybody was highly nervous. Many of them had seen towns taken over by soldiers decked with red ribbons and hundreds of their relatives had been shot. Everyone we met seemed to have lost a husband, son or brother, and most of them all their worldly possessions.

'They didnae tell us this part o' the deal,' Munro observed.

I shrugged. 'You can't expect politicians to be *that* honest,' I said. 'After all, Lloyd George said we were fighting the war in France to make a land fit for heroes to live in, but they were already talking when we left about a slump and people being unemployed.'

We were given billets of appalling discomfort with no transport, no orderlies and no interpreters. The languid types from Batum were here, too, and equally discouraging.

'Avoid the Front at all costs,' they advised. 'The Russians are riddled with typhus and if you go up there you'll get it too, and then you're sure to die. Besides, you can never tell when they won't turn round and shoot you in the back. A lot of them have already done it to their own officers so there's no reason why they shouldn't do it to you.'

It sounded a cheerful prospect.

'Of course—' the speaker was a portly lieutenant from the Ordnance Corps '—we learned how to handle these types in France.' He looked at the furry moustache I was trying to grow, despite all Sykes' warnings, on my upper lip to make me look a little older. 'But you're only a boy. You won't have seen much of the war.'

I felt myself going red with anger, but Munro merely grinned. 'Let me tak' y'r coat, Brat,' he suggested.

'I'll keep it on. It's not all that warm.'

'Och, Ah can see ye sweatin'.'

Then I realized what he was getting at. I was wearing a heavy khaki mackintosh without rank badges, and I grinned back at him and started to unbutton it.

'You soon get into the way of things, of course,' the Ordnance Corps officer was saying. 'It won't take you long.'

Then, as Munro wrenched off the mackintosh with much more alacrity than he need have done, he saw the crowns on my shoulders and the wings and the ribbons on my chest and he swallowed the drink he was holding in his hand and hurriedly disappeared.

Munro gave a yell of laughter. 'Mon, if his een had stuck out any further they'd hae rolled on the floor like marbles!'

Sykes was up near Ekaterinodar and the squadron ground staff, guards and several of the pilots were at Debaltsevo. The rest of us were arriving in odd lots as we were released from hospital, home squadrons, the Middle East and desk jobs at the Air Ministry. Munro and I had first-class tickets but we travelled in a third-class carriage that was dirty, cushionless and cold and looked as though it had been in use at the time of the

Crimean War. All its fittings, windows and brass-work were out of date and the seats were merely hard benches, but the third-class passengers were far worse off in carriages known as *terplushkas* that were nothing more than freight cars with a brazier inside for them for the winter. They were crowded inside and outside with people, feather beds, pots and pans and, though the big engine was streaming smoke from its funnel-shaped stack and the driver was in the cab adjusting the valves so that I expected to leave at once, it was ages before we finally drew out of the station.

With us we had an ex-Russian Imperial Air Force officer with what appeared to be an unpro-nounceable name. As we grew used to it, it turned out to be Alexei Ivanovitch Yazheskov-Pudhovkhin, but he didn't seem to mind a bit when we shortened it to 'Puddy'. He was a baron and had won the Cross of St George, Tsarist Russia's highest military honour, flying against the Austrians and Germans – mostly in out-of-date, badly serviced machines – and had escaped from the revolution to the Middle East where he'd flown for a while with the RAF. From there he'd returned to Russia to join the White Army and, because he'd picked up a little English, was joining us as an interpreter.

He was a lean good-looking man with perfect manners and a constant smile, and officially he wasn't supposed to fly because Sykes had decided that if he had to force-land and was captured by the Bolsheviks his life wouldn't be worth a fig.

'But I fly, just the same,' he said with a smile. 'I have machine, you see. Albatros. German machine. It has Mercedes engine and many horses. It fly very well. I turn the spanners myself. Is better this way because Russian mechanics know damn nothing.'

In the circumstances it was obviously going to be difficult to keep him on the ground because his one desire was to smite the Bolsheviks hip and thigh and bring back – if not the Tsar, of whom, apparently, he'd never had a very high opinion – then at least some sort of stability. He was the very best type of Russian officer, straightforward, good-humoured and with a rigid sense of honour; but also with that strange streak of melancholy in his make-up so many Russians seem to have – emotional, too conscious of the inevitability of fate, a little obsessed with death, and convinced that, although they'd replace the hated revolution with a system that would be freer than the old autocratic system of the Tsars, he would never live to see it.

Because he believed it was his fate, it didn't worry him. 'It is written in the book,' he said. 'I am doomed. All my friends are doomed. Perhaps you also are doomed,' he ended cheerfully.

Munro glared at him, unable to understand such fatalism. Munro had survived more disasters than anyone I knew and he still managed to be aggressively cheerful about it.

'Ah dinnae ken what *you* think,' he said hotly, 'but Ah'm no' doomed.'

Pudhovkhin smiled. He was a remarkably good-looking man and his smile was sweet and understanding. 'What you do not realize, Sir Captain,' he explained, 'is that fate has a habit of creeping up on you when you are not looking.'

Munro snorted. 'It had better no' creep up too close,' he growled, 'or it'll get a kick in the teeth.'

—

The journey was slow and each time we stopped to take on fuel, everybody climbed down to buy roast chickens from the peasants, post letters home, or collect water from the station for washing or making tea in their portable samovars; while the children played games alongside the track, the wealthy walked their pet dogs, and the women changed their clothing. At Ekaterinodar there was no sign of Sykes and we were pushed into an empty boys' school with no more comfort than a wooden bed and an army blanket. It was all a bit different from the flying messes in France which, even in the worst days, we'd managed to make homes from home. There wasn't even any food so that we had to buy our own at a scruffy restaurant down the road. Mostly it consisted of grey bread, grey omelettes and grey tea.

'Ah'm beginnin' tae think,' Munro said, 'that it's no' goin' tae be quite as we expected – nor even as Sykes – or for that matter, the government – expected.'

I had a feeling he might be right and certainly the area round Ekaterinodar didn't suggest stability, comfort or order. Many of the buildings around us, like the one we were in, were marked by the fighting of the last twelve months and the countryside around was full of deserted, half-burnt villages and wrecked stations where occasionally the yellow-and-black striped posts with the old double-headed eagle of Tsarist Russia could still be seen alongside the signpost giving the name of the place and its population. Shutters creaked and gates rattled untended, and many of the houses were marked by huge scorch marks where the flames had caught them.

Three days later Sykes turned up, driving a Stutz that didn't seem terribly reliable despite the fact that it looked big enough to haul a string of railway waggons. He was full of apologies for the way we'd been treated but he'd been up to Debaltsevo trying to set the base there in order. With him was an enormous youngster with the shoulders of an ox and great fists like coal grabs. Judging by his accent he was an American from one of the Southern states but he wore RAF uniform and wings and the two pips of a lieutenant.

'This – all of it—' Sykes introduced '—is Stuart Lee Tucker, junior, known inevitably as "Tommy". He's one of our pilots.'

Munro stared. 'They never get yon lump intae a Camel, do they?' he said.

The giant grinned. 'Sure do,' he said.

'Probably noticed,' Sykes said. 'He's a Yank—'

'No, *sir!*' Tucker grinned. 'I'm from El Paso, Texas, and it just isn't done to refer to a true-believin', God-fearin' Texan as a "Yank".'

Sykes smiled. 'Came over to England with a Canadian outfit in 1917. Managed to fly with 44 Squadron during the last two months of the war. Just long enough to get him interested. Think he's a sabotage agent, actually, still carrying on the War of Independence. He crashed his Camel yesterday.'

'These colonials,' I said.

Despite his smiles, Sykes seemed a little worried, and he explained that since meeting the Russians he'd come to the conclusion that someone, either in Russia or in London, had put one across us, because the Whites seemed to be hopelessly disorganized and not very efficient and he didn't rate their chances quite as high as he had in England.

By this time, we were beginning to understand what he meant.

The ordinary Russian soldiers we'd met were mostly awkward youths from steppe villages who had a tendency to tie flowers to the barrels of their rifles, gape at large brick buildings and even weep with fear at the sight of a train. Yet, despite their

35

backwardness, they seemed willing enough and it was their officers who were hopeless. Dressed in a mixture of uniforms which included button boots and grey flannels or elaborate breeches of extraordinary cut, and badges of rank marked with blue pencil, they were generous to the point of absurdity but useless in every other way except to swear dreadful oaths of revenge on the Bolsheviks and join societies with terrifying names that had no meaning whatsoever. They couldn't get things done and we often saw them riding while their wounded walked. They were lazy, pessimistic, boastful, ignorant, inefficient, untidy, untruthful and dishonest. Some were even downright opportunist, grabbing everything they could without the slightest intention of taking their units anywhere near the Bolsheviks. Considering that many of their recruits had probably once already changed sides overnight and shot their officers in the back, perhaps they had a point.

As he drove us out of town to an aerodrome at Chernomorkst, Sykes seemed to cheer up.

'News is good, though,' he said. 'That's one thing.' He stopped the car to indicate a huge map on the wall of a shop, marked with red lines to show the Front, which was surrounded by a crowd of gaping people. 'Those things are everywhere,' he pointed out. 'To give everybody hope. The whole of the northern Caucasus is in Denikin's pocket already, Wrangel's just liberated the Terek region, and Kolchak's on the march towards Moscow. Might be spending Christmas in the Kremlin yet. Collishaw's at Beketofka and we're all just waiting for the mud to dry a little so we can start operations. You'll be living in a train.'

'A train, f'r God's sake!' Munro wailed.

'Very comfortable,' Sykes said. 'And the only way to do it. This is a cavalry war and we'll be too much on the move to have a permanent base. When the planes aren't flying, they'll be on the train, too. Your landing fields will be the steppes right alongside. Getting the picture?'

Munro looked a little stunned and Sykes continued. 'You fly up to Debaltsevo tomorrow. B Flight's already up there. I'll join you later in the day with C Flight train.'

The train, where we dumped our kit, consisted of an engine and tender, two Pullman cars, a lounge-mess car and twenty-five box freights, *terplushkas* and flat cars. The pilots' quarters were in the Pullmans, and in the *terplushkas* were the ground crews, soldiers assigned as guards and a few prisoners of war who acted as batmen. The flat cars were to carry the aircraft and the box cars the workshops, ammunition, oil and provisions.

We took off after dawn next morning, me in front, with Munro to one side, and Tommy Tucker and Yazheskov-Pudhovkhin on the other. As always I was impressed with what a splendid machine the Camel was. Snub-nosed, with none of the graceful lines of an SE, it still had a clean workmanlike look about it and was twice as exciting to fly. Inexperienced pilots hated Camels as much as *they* hated inexperienced pilots. Unstable and tail-heavy, they were so light on the controls the slightest jerk would hurl them all over the sky. They were difficult to land, deadly to crash and had a list of vices that was enough to make the stoutest heart quail, but flying them was like controlling a typhoon and, if attacked, you could do incredible things with them. They were awkward and dangerous but they suited my temperament exactly and I'd loved them from the first day I'd set eyes on them.

It was obviously easier to follow the railway line than go in for clever navigational workings, but the steppe looked bare and chilly and depressingly empty of life. The few villages we saw only served to make the monotony seem worse because they all looked exactly alike, with square, thatched houses the colour of mud, among them always two churches – Russian Orthodox with white walls and a green roof and gables, and Moslem with a red roof and a dome.

When the railway looped round a village, as it did occasionally, we merely crossed the ends, and just about the time when fuel was beginning to run low, we lost Tucker, who moved up alongside me, waggled his wings and pointed to his engine to indicate he was having trouble. A moment later, he swung away and down and I saw him make a landing miles from anywhere. It was impossible to fix a navigational point in that vast empty land, but I checked the name of the last village with the map and when we came into the aerodrome at Debaltsevo it wasn't hard to indicate where he was.

The flight-sergeant who took my directions was a broad-shouldered smiling man well-named Merry. He was quite unperturbed. 'No trouble at all, sir,' he said. 'We'll send out a DH9 with spare parts and a mechanic. He'll be here in no time.'

The hangars were the old Bessonneaux type from France, but the countryside was about as unlike France as it was possible to be, stretching away to infinity, grey-brown and full of nothing.

Munro had climbed from his cockpit first and he appeared at my side as I sat staring at it. He seemed startled.

'Big, is it no'?' he said.

'It is a bit,' I agreed.

'Plenty o' elbow room, though, mon. Room tae move.'

After France and the crowded land of England, the sheer size was unnerving. It was almost as if no one had ever been there before we'd arrived, and only that shining double steel rail curving between the rising and falling ground indicated that they had.

'One thing,' Munro said. 'Ah willnae need tae worry aboot bumpin' intae ye as we're taxiing.'

As I climbed from the cockpit I was aware of a strange feeling of emptiness and loneliness that I put down to the immensity of the landscape and I began to see the reason for that famous gloom

Russian authors have always written about. The evening haze was caught weakly in the undergrowth near the river, purple-coloured through the weeds rustling in the breeze that had risen to lick the edges of the plain, and everything was totally silent except for the click and creak of cooling engines and the jingle of bits as a troop of cavalry trotted past, huddled in their saddles.

'It's damn big, isn't it?' Munro muttered again, staring round him uneasily.

'You should see Texas,' Tommy said.

Munro gestured, recovering his spirits at once. 'Mice as big as cats, cats as big as horses, an' horses as big as you.' He stared at the steppes again. 'It's so still,' he said.

And it *was* still. There was no sound. Not a bird. Not a movement. Just the rustle of the reeds and the faint click of the cavalrymen's hooves dying away in the distance.

The other pilots seemed a good mixture – all experienced flyers with sound records, though James Alonzo St John Slingsby, as Sykes had suggested, was as mad as a March hare. He was a languid young man with some of Sykes' manner but, instead of Sykes' good looks, he was pale to the point of anonymity, with pale hair, pale skin and pale eyes. There was nothing pale about his personality, however, or his flying, and despite the innocent expression he wore, when I sent him up to see what he could do, it was obvious he had no nerves at all. As I watched him doing wingtip turns just above the ground with the Camel as steady as if it were on rails, I decided that, if nothing else, he knew his business.

'I never did like manoeuvring at nought feet,' Munro observed gravely. 'The wet grass gets in the way a wee bit.'

'Tray bon aviayteur,' Slingsby said in atrocious French as he climbed down. 'Tray beeang aylevay in the air.'

He did look younger than I did and he was certainly madder, claiming five Germans shot down in France and one knocked off his horse with his wheels.

'Of course, he *was* on a hill,' he admitted modestly. 'And the silly ass would insist on shooting at me when I had no ammunition left.' He grinned, his eyes full of excitement and humour. 'Always go a bit mad in a Camel, y'see. It's because I started on RE8s and if you were daring enough in one of those to put on more than forty-five degrees of bank you were in a spin at once and it took five minutes' struggling with the controls and a special incantation to get it out again.'

He seemed, when we sat down to dinner, to have an appetite for about seven men which went oddly with his slender frame and cherub-like face, and he seemed to have decided at once that Munro was a good butt for his odd sense of humour. He also seemed to have a gift for sleight of hand and afterwards gave us all an impromptu performance with the salt cellar, the pepper pot and Munro's glass of whisky.

'Ye're dicin' wi' death, mon, doin' that,' Munro warned. 'Y'oughta know that a Scotsman's whisky's sacred. In the regiment Ah sairved wi' before Ah joined this outfit, ye'd hae been drummed oot, cashiered and probably hanged, drawn an' quartered for that.'

In a siding nearby there was a Russian squadron with their own trains, their machines marked with the red, black and white rondels of the White forces. Their bombers were British DH9s which were well-designed aeroplanes and an improved version of the old DH4. The petrol tanks which had separated the pilot and observer by so much space they could never communicate with each other had been shifted and they had good lines, but their BHP engines were still appallingly undependable. In France they'd caused more losses than enemy bullets and they required a great deal of careful servicing that somehow I didn't think the Russians would be capable of. They also had a few other mixed types including an ancient Caudron pusher, a BE2, three battered-looking Nieuports and six Morane monoplanes. In 1916 the Moranes had been considered the 'cleanest' aircraft in service, with a single wing braced with wires from kingposts above and below. With their streamlined propeller boss, they'd acquired the name 'Bullets' and they'd helped to defeat the Fokker scourge, but 1916 was a long time ago in terms of aircraft development so that I didn't give them much of a chance because the Bolsheviks were said to possess Fokker DVIIs, triplanes and Albatroses which they'd acquired from the Germans.

The Moranes were decorated with skulls and crossbones and on some of them were words in Cyrillic letters which Pudhovkhin told us meant things like 'The Avenger' and 'Death to the

Bolsheviks'. It all seemed rather childish and melo-dramatic and not quite what would have been approved of by the Royal Air Force which had even objected to coloured cowlings and wheel hubs at a time when we were being dazzled cross-eyed by the Richthofen Circus's gaudy paintwork.

'Is very Russian,' Pudhovkhin explained. 'Russians think much about death and fate.'

'If y'ask me, mon,' Munro said, 'Ah think they think too damn much. In fact, where Ah come from ony feller who went on like you, wid be asking for a poke in the ee tae wake him up. 'Tis an auld custom aroond Aberdeen. Very Scottish, ye ken.'

Pudhovkhin saw the joke and grinned. 'When that happens here, Sir Captain,' he said, 'sometimes they get a poke back. This is also the custom. Very Cossack, you understand.'

—

Because they were technicians, the Russian airmen were a cut above the army types we'd seen, but even so they still had the same indifferent attitude to work and I couldn't imagine that they were over-efficient. One or two of them had clearly joined the Air Force for the kudos it gave them and they wore perfume and skin-tight breeches. Pudhovkhin didn't think much of them.

Sykes arrived the following day with the train and we left the aerodrome to operate on our own further west. Since much of the Russian railway system consisted of a single track, there were loop lines every few miles where trains could wait so that another coming in the opposite direction could pass, and it was from these that we were to operate.

Sykes had brought a letter from Charley. 'Dearest Martin,' she said, 'I think I've been diddled. I've learned through one of the Sykeses' numerous connections at the War Office that you're not in Russia to instruct as I thought, but to *FIGHT!!!!!*' This word was written in thick capitals, underlined and followed by a string of exclamations marks. 'I suppose,' she went on, 'that I should have no fear, despite this horrifying news, because your head seems to be harder than your engines, and I have a feeling inside me that you'll come back somehow, full of dudgeon as always, your indignation at being caught worth a guinea a box. All the same, I'll be praying a bit.' She signed it, 'All my love, Charley' which was reassuring and warming, and for good measure she included a new photograph of herself on a horse taken by one of the society magazines while out with the Quorn. 'The one on top's me,' she'd written across it.

It made me laugh and left me feeling happy, but Sykes had bad news, too. French troops had been defeated by the Bolsheviks near Kherson and had sailed for Odessa. 'Suspect they're getting out,' he said.

'There were a lot of Communists in Paris after the war,' Tucker pointed out. 'Mebbe it kinda makes intervention a bit embarrassing.'

'Or impossible.' Munro spoke with the pomposity of a bishop, as he always did when he felt he knew something no one else did. 'Ah haird that Lloyd George thinks the Whites havenae got a chance.'

'Then why the blazes did he send us out here?' Jasper said. 'Personally, I'd trust Lloyd George as far as I could throw him. That gang he formed his government from were a hard-faced lot who looked as though they'd done pretty well out of the war.'

'He reckons it would take four hundred thousand British soldiers,' Munro went on.

'Told you himself, I suppose?' I asked.

Munro's steam pressure was already dangerously high and he had never kept out of an argument in his life. They were meat and drink to him and he sailed in now with all his guns going in a broadside of contempt.

'Ah'm a Liberal too,' he explained, as if that meant he had the ear of the Prime Minister. 'An' Ah agree wi' him because too many folk back home think intervention in Russia's an unjustifiable adventure which adds hardship tae the population and has no object except tae replace the Tsars.'

'You inclined to Communism, Jock?' Slingsby asked.

'No. Ah'm just a realist and Ah'm beginning tae think we've been landed wi' somethin' that hasnae a cat in hell's chance o' succeeding.'

'Rubbish,' Tucker said. 'We shall be in Moscow by Christmas, man.'

Munro refused to be convinced. 'That's what they all say. But they're forgetting yon feller, Trotsky, who's quite a performer as Minister o' War. An' they're also forgettin' that the Bolshies hae the one thing that the Whites dinnae have – a goal. They want a new world. The Whites just want the old one. And yon's dead. It's even dead in England.'

I'd expected that now we had our aeroplanes, our pilots and our train, that we'd start operations at once, but it wasn't to be as simple as that.

'Been told to put on a bit of a show to help morale,' Sykes explained. 'Big parade in the city tomorrow, and we've been told by British Mission headquarters that our presence there will cheer everybody up. Tell the chaps to get out the boot-brushes and buttonsticks.'

Debaltsevo looked even shabbier than Ekaterinodar because of the see-saw fighting in the area the previous year. Windows were boarded up and deep gouges were cut in the plaster by bullets and shrapnel, while hammers and sickles had been painted on doors and there were a few posters – 'War To The Finish' and 'Death Is Better Than Slavery' – but since they appeared to apply to both sides, it was hard to tell who'd put them there.

There were three batteries of artillery drawn up outside the cathedral, with two or three regiments of Cossacks, dramatic, fierce-looking men on shaggy ponies, with long lovelocks of hair curled Cossack-fashion over the left ear. They seemed surprised that we hadn't brought our aeroplanes with us and it took a little doing to convince them that it was difficult to move aeroplanes in formation with horses and guns.

They'd brought their horse-tail regimental standards and an altar had been erected; and priests in glittering robes and surrounded by acolytes performed their offices to the sound of the cathedral bells. The solemnity of the service was intensified by huge crucifixes and the bass voices of the choir in Gregorian chants. The *Te Deum* was followed by the presentation of flags and, as our banner changed hands, Tommy Tucker, who, because he was the biggest and most impressive-looking, had been delegated to receive it, dropped on one knee. There were more rumbled prayers, a sermon and more choral singing, and enough holy water flung about by the Bishop's whisk among the rising blue smoke from the censers to give us all a good bath, and then everybody marched past the saluting base. As the Cossacks cantered off, they broke into song, their officers conducting the singing with their whips from the front.

It was an impressive enough ceremony but it was a world away from the war in France and for the most part far above our heads. For one thing the religion was Russian Orthodox and for another we didn't understand much of what was going on.

'The Bishop say,' Pudhovkhin translated, 'that we shall prevail because God is on our side.'

Munro wasn't impressed. 'Ah reckon,' he whispered to me, 'that God's been on a lot o' sides in the last few years, sometimes two at once.'

He stared at the banner, his face puzzled. It was a beautiful piece of work, specially embroidered by the ladies of the city for us, but we didn't know what to do with it because the RAF had never gone in much for flags.

'We could always give it to Flight-Sergeant Merry,' Slingsby said. 'Torn up it would make good rags for the flight mechs.'

Two days later, with Sykes back in Ekat rounding up the last of our pilots, we took off on our first patrol. We got up in the darkness and I could hear voices coming from the other compartments as we struggled with clothing and equipment.

'What the hell are you washing for?' Slingsby was demanding of Tucker in his high, pale voice.

'Because I'm not a dirty pig like you,' Tommy snorted.

'Half an hour after take-off you'll be covered with castor oil and if you're killed, what'll be the point?'

'At least they'll be able to bury me clean. My mother always used to insist on me wearing fresh underclothes when I went out in case I was run over.'

The cook had provided boiled eggs, tea and toast. For some reason all dawn patrols started with boiled eggs, and they were always hard, and Slingsby was staring at his in disgust.

'Toojoors dure,' he mourned. 'Always hard. Why do we always have *hardboiled* eggs?'

'What would you like?' I asked. 'Hardboiled caviare?'

'Can't see why not? It's only eggs, after all – fishes' eggs.'

As we climbed down from the train and headed for the machines, the first of the DH9s took off. They were there to bomb Bolshevik bases towards Kharkov and provide support for the Royal Navy and Russian gunboats in the Sea of Azov near Taganrog.

One after the other they rolled across the uneven surface of the steppe. They were sturdy-looking machines which had done well as bombers in France with the Independent Air Force – the only unit, in fact, apart from the Royal Navy with its blockade, which had carried the war to the untouched German homeland. The wide wings rocked, the sun catching the doped fabric stretched across their ribs and spars, and we followed them soon afterwards, bouncing through the grass, the machines rattling and clattering until the wheels left and the last rumbling stopped as we became airborne in snarling, hissing little fabric-covered boxes dragged along by their huge rotary engines.

As we climbed, we could see Slavyansk sprawling below us and then barbed wire and trenches so that I immediately began to think of France. The Red Army's anti-aircraft guns started. They were obviously using old German shells left over from the war, with the usual dense black smoke, and the first one that exploded nearby made me jump as they always did. The gunners weren't very good, though, and we didn't bother to dodge.

We'd lost Stagg with engine trouble within ten minutes of taking off and then my own engine started missing, picking up again and faltering once more, so that I began to pray it wouldn't conk completely and deposit me behind the Red Army lines. The Bolsheviks appeared to have a few nasty habits towards prisoners and at Tsaritsyn were said to have murdered twelve thousand civilians when they'd captured the place.

One minute the engine seemed to be pulling well so that I felt I ought to continue, but the next it was spluttering so much I had to lean heavily on the fuel pump, and in the end, I decided there was no sense in taking risks and signed to Munro to take over. He waved back and I swung southwards towards Debaltsevo.

To the south of Slavyansk as I headed home, I saw a flight of Nieuports heading towards me. After four years of fighting Fokkers and Albatroses, I automatically thought 'friends' and took no evading action. Then I saw Fokker triplanes, too, and since they all seemed very matey, forming up in formation on each other, I looked again and it suddenly dawned on me that they all wore red stars on their wings and fuselages. It was then I remembered that the Red Air Force also included machines the Russians had collected from the Allies during the war, and you could no longer rely on a silhouette to give you an identity.

I whipped round in the cockpit to watch them, well aware that neither a Nieuport nor a Tripe could touch a Camel when it was in good shape, but then the engine coughed and I remembered that mine *wasn't* in good shape. They seemed to sense I was in trouble because they came for me like a pack of ravening wolves and, as they drew nearer, I experienced the usual sweating apprehension that I'd never managed to cure – the same sort of dread you fear before stepping into the sea on a bitter day. It required an effort, but I knew that as soon as I was involved it would be all right.

Because of the trouble with the engine I kept heading south, one eye always over my shoulder, and eventually one of the Nieuports dropped into place on my tail. I had a trick worth two of that, though, and swung the Camel into a roll and, laying the machine flat against the air in a vertical bank, slipped neatly behind the Nieuport as it shot past. The Russian pilot's head turned and I was close enough to see the look of horror on his face. If he'd been on his own I might have let him go, because it wasn't my war despite what they said in London, but there were already three more machines elbowing each other out of the way to get behind me, and I had to fire.

Nieuports always had a nasty habit of stripping their wings and this one was no exception. They folded back with a bang I could hear even over my own engine and the machine disappeared below me, with that rare dramatic beauty of a sinking ship on its last plunge beneath the sea. It was never pleasant to think of killing a human being and the thrill of the chase was always more stimulating than the end, but it was also never possible to divorce yourself entirely from that tremendous and tragic excitement of a downed machine and, leaning over the edge of the cockpit, I saw the Nieuport dwindling beneath me, dropping in a steep, erratic curve.

The disaster seemed to have startled the rest of the Red pilots with its suddenness because they drew off a little. Deciding – if their leader were any indication of what the rest of them were like – that attack would be the best form of defence, I snatched the Camel round in a vertical bank, and went at them like a bat out of hell. They scattered across the sky like a flock of frightened birds.

They were back immediately, though, but they were trying to shoot at me as if I were flying a stationary-engined aeroplane and that was always a mistake with a Camel because it was never going the way it seemed to be going. Camels even took off sideways if you let them and in a dogfight they could be going in any direction imaginable except backwards, and nothing in the sky could turn as tightly, so that if you were in trouble all you had to do was put it into a tight bank and keep on turning until the other chap got bored and went home.

By the grace of God my engine was having one of its periods of running well and the Russians weren't all that good and after one or two half-hearted potshots at me, they decided they'd taken on something that didn't play fair and broke off the fight to dive away to the north. As they disappeared I decided I'd better head for safety, too, and as I swung away I saw the Nieuport I'd shot down burning on the edge of a lake.

When the others returned I was eating hard-boiled eggs and spring onions. They'd also seen the burning machine and Munro looked at me as if I'd committed a crime.

'As Ah was comin' back,' he said slowly. 'Ah saw an aeroplane burning by a lake. It looked tae me like a Nieuport.'

'And it looked as if dire things had been happening to it,' Slingsby grinned. 'As if the archangels had sounded the trump of doom over it, as you might say.'

Munro stared at me. 'Would *you* know onythin' aboot it?'

'Yes, I would,' I said. 'A bit.'

'Just wound up the alarm clock and went to sleep, I suppose,' Slingsby said, 'while he flew round and shot himself down.'

'You know damn well that a Nieuport's no match for a Camel,' Munro accused.

'He started it.'

'Ye're naethin' but a big bully!'

'I was quietly coming home,' I protested. 'I'd have been quite happy to have gone on my way but he insisted on shoving his long nose into my business.'

'So ye did for him?'

'It was him or me.'

The others were grinning all over their faces now and Munro turned to them and spread his arms wide.

'God spare ma belly an' teeth,' he said in disgust. 'If some ham-fisted Russian farmhand who's been shoved intae an aeroplane decides tae make a fight o' it an' goes round beggin' tae be shot doon, ye can bet y'r last dollar that he'll pick on yon baby-faced brute. He's already got so many they ought tae make him a general.'

Everybody was noisily cheerful but, as we reached the train, Flight-Sergeant Merry produced a message from Sykes in Ekaterinodar to say that the French government really had got cold feet about intervention and were pulling out of Russia. The French commander at Odessa had even received orders to get his troops out of the Black Sea in three days and the civilian population, terrified of being caught by avenging Red troops when they swept down on the evacuated port, had panicked and there had been a wave of suicides which was affecting White morale even in Ekaterinodar.

'I guess it'll affect 'em up here, too, when they find out,' Tommy Tucker said grimly.

The excitement of the squadron's first victory in Russia was lost in the gloom, and it was typical of Munro that he found the answer.

'Only one thing tae do,' he said.

'What's that?'

'Same as we always do when the news is bad,' Slingsby yelled, catching his mood. 'Have a party!'

Pudhovkhin was just about to set off for the Russian squadron's train to invite a few men he knew when a message arrived to say that the general commanding the Debaltsevo area had also learned of our first victory and suggested that we should attend a party he was giving to a few visiting bigwigs in the city.

'Och, weel,' Munro grinned. 'Any Scot would go for that, because we willnae be payin'.'

The 'party' was larger than we'd expected and turned out, in fact, to be one of the jaunts that the White Army commanders always seemed to be throwing. With all the candelabra and waiters, it looked to me more like a banquet, and as we walked into the reception we were awed by the number of cars and carriages waiting outside. We had no idea what the rules of protocol were – and we knew they were always very rigid – and into the bargain we felt a little drab in our khaki, because the other guests hadn't spared a thing. They appeared in blazing uniforms, studded with decorations and glittering with jewels, epaulettes, brilliant sword hilts and polished boots until it looked like the ball in Brussels before Waterloo. There must have been around a hundred generals there, to say nothing of men and women who'd been members of Moscow and Petrograd society and close to the Tsar; refugee members of the old Russian parliament; government officials; church dignitaries, including the Bishop – in full robes! – to pronounce a blessing, and at the end of the hall, a full Cossack choir to sing a choral grace.

Only Munro's kilt saved the day for us because, like the service we'd attended, it was a long way from the sort of war we'd got used to in France, and seemed like part of another world and another century.

'Mon—' Munro was awed almost to the point of speechlessness, which, for Munro, was quite something '—Ah didnae know we were attending a *levée*.'

The introductions, which seemed to consist of shaking hands with everyone in the room, were alarming, and we were way out of our depth as most of the conversation had to be conducted through an interpreter and there weren't many of them. Those of us who'd learned French during the war were a little better off because a lot of the educated Russians spoke it too, but, although everyone was very noisy, despite the cheerfulness I noticed odd little gaps in the conversation, hastily covered with a quick smile, which seemed to indicate more than anything how the circumstances of most of the guests had changed. The talk was wistful, the women sighing for pretty clothes which were not only unobtainable but for the first time in their lives entirely beyond their means. After a while I was quite lost and could only remember being introduced to two or three princesses and several countesses. Baronesses seemed to be two a penny, and I wondered what on earth they were all doing, because none of them seemed to be helping the White cause. They didn't even seem to have their feet on the earth and appeared to be just waiting for a return to the old days which anyone with an ounce of sense could see were never going to come back.

The affair seemed to run chiefly on Crimean wine and nostalgia but as the evening got going, the toasts – always including '*Na Moskvu*', 'To Moscow' – came faster and faster as the music from twanging balalaikas and beribboned accordions grew louder. Finally one of the Russian pilots who'd been working hard all night at the Abrau

Durso, the Tsarist champagne, simply slid out of sight behind a table. No one turned a hair and the woman next to me, who'd been introduced as Princess Irene Something-or-other, beamed cheerfully. 'How wonderful,' she said gaily. 'It is in *such* a good cause!'

The food consisted of *hors-d'œuvres* which were a meal in themselves, caviare of all sorts, radishes, hot slices of mutton, pancakes covered with white sauces and kidneys cooked in some kind of peppery juice. Slingsby thoroughly enjoyed himself, much to Munro's disapproval.

'Yon stuff's too hot,' he said. 'Ye'll ruin the linin' o' y'r stomach.'

Slingsby grinned. 'I'm trying to, old boy. Pass that plate, will you?'

The dancing consisted chiefly of mazurkas, which left us blank, but occasionally we got going in a polka or a waltz and once, as a sop to the younger people, an unexpected Bunny Hug. There were a few nurses present in uniform but, because they were working for the war, all the Russian men seemed to prefer to pay attention to the other women and girls; and, partly because they seemed a little left out of things, partly because we felt we'd have no need to be over-awed by them, we decided to join them.

In no time at all Slingsby had their eyes popping out of their heads as he produced hardboiled eggs – deftly removed from the tables – from behind their ears and out of their hair, and Munro had grabbed one of them and was dancing in a curious sort of hop, skip and jump step which, even if it wasn't exactly elegant, at least got him around. The girl he was with was dark with huge eyes. She was small with fine bones and a beautiful head and because she was slender she looked taller than she was and she was staring at Munro in bewilderment.

Eventually I found myself in a corner with her doing the wooden-legged act which normally passed with me for dancing and chattering away in the happy understanding that she couldn't make out a word I was saying. She was quiet and shy and listened carefully as I spoke, in a way I assumed was Russian politeness.

'It's a nice dance,' I observed cheerfully.

She didn't answer and I went on, putting on a show of polite chit-chat with no real expectation of any return beyond, perhaps, a smile. 'Everybody's here,' I said. 'The general. The butcher, the baker, the candlestick maker. And if you ask me they all have rather a high opinion of themselves.'

'Please?'

'All these people,' I said. 'All dressed up and nowhere to go. Adding nothing to the war effort except their smiles. Mind, they do say you get introduced to a princess for shooting down the first Bolshevik plane.'

Her eyebrows shot up. 'You are the one which have shot a Bolshevik aeroplane?' she said.

I was so startled I lost the step. Since I was the sort of dancer who had to say 'one, two, three, hop' to myself to put on any sort of show at all, it brought us to a full stop and she smiled gravely.

'I think you do not dance good,' she said.

'No,' I agreed. 'I do *not* dance good. And you startled me. I didn't think you spoke English.'

'Oh, yes,' she said. 'Of course. I have an English governess, you see, and I also learn at the Smolnia, which is the very best girls' school in Petrograd.'

'You didn't speak English to Munro,' I pointed out.

She frowned. 'Who is this Munro?'

I indicated Munro still gallantly jigging round in his kilt with one of the other nurses. 'That's Munro.

65

The little chap with a face that looks as though it's been run over. Actually, it has.'

She looked puzzled. 'But this Munro is not English surely?' she said.

'Of course he is.'

'But he does not speak English to *me*. I think perhaps he is Hungarian or perhaps a Pole or a Greek.'

I hooted with laughter and she looked worried. 'Perhaps I have said the mistake,' she suggested.

'No,' I grinned. 'You have not said the mistake. And I suppose he isn't English after all. He's a Scot. They're a sort of hairy type of dwarf who live in the north of the British Isles. They wear skirts, drink firewater and are given to uttering loud yelps when they dance.'

She clearly didn't understand me so I explained it more carefully and much more slowly and very soon she was leaning against me, weak with laughter. I'd never realized before that I was funny.

'I think perhaps you will not be introduced to a princess this time,' she said. 'And perhaps your friend Munro will not either, because I think we have almost run out of princesses. Perhaps you will have to be content with something less.'

'Nothing less than a princess,' I said firmly. 'The country's stiff with countesses and as for baronesses—'

'What is wrong with baronesses?' she said.

I was aware of a sudden chill in the air and when, at that moment, the dancing stopped we left the floor in silence. She disappeared soon afterwards with the other nurses and I was so puzzled I sought out Pudhovkhin and asked him if I'd said something wrong.

'I think you do,' he grinned.

'Why? Has she got something against baronesses or something?'

'No. Other way, I think. Her name, you see, Sir Major, is the same as mine. It is Olga Pudhovkhina. *Baroness* Olga Pudhovkhina. She is my little sister, Olga Ivanovna.'

Chapter 3

Since I was supposed to be running the show when Sykes wasn't around, it seemed to be up to me to do something about apologizing. From Pudhovkhin, I found that the nurses had all come from a hospital train in one of the sidings nearby which I discovered was identified only as 'Train Number 643'. Since writing was difficult, as it might well move before a letter was delivered, I went to look for it.

The Russian squadron train was standing in the siding with its Moranes lined up on the steppe with their British de Havillands. They told me the hospital train had left for the Tsaritsyn Front and the commander of the Russian squadron, a scented gentleman by the name of Rhatanyi, said they were expecting to follow. There was trouble brewing between Denikin and Wrangel, it seemed. Denikin was being pushed by Wrangel to drive for Tsaritsyn, join Kolchak and head for Moscow along the Volga but he preferred not to separate his troops and was ignoring the suggestion. The squadron mess car contained a piano, wickerwork chairs and pot plants so that it looked like a Victorian drawing room, and the walls were decorated with pictures, chiefly of coy-looking ladies, cut from magazines or painted by the officers themselves. At one end were four or five Russian girls, all very well dressed, one of them playing a balalaika.

'They are all married to our officers,' Rhatanyi said. 'All except one and she will be married soon.'

It was far from unusual to find girls on the Russian military trains. They were employed in various ways – as clerks and cooks, sometimes just to look pretty and cheer up the officers – but unfortunately, the generals worried about them being captured by the Reds so that they wouldn't take their trains anywhere that looked dangerous and tried to do their commanding from a point miles behind the line. It seemed a funny way to run a war and I couldn't imagine that it helped towards efficiency.

I hadn't realized it, but it seemed that Tucker had also noticed Olga Pudhovkhina. Despite his size, however, for an American he was surprisingly shy with girls. His share of the dancing had been very formal and sedate and it seemed that he'd watched Olga Pudhovkhina with longing throughout the evening and had already developed a doglike devotion for her. It was only when he brought up the subject that I realized what he'd been feeling.

'The *baryshnia* with the big eyes,' he said. 'The one you and Jock were dancing with.'

'What about her?'

'Oh, boy!' He seemed unable to say more in his tongue-tied emotion.

'You look as if you'd been hit on the head with a croquet mallet,' I said.

'Say l'amoor,' Slingsby pointed out. 'The bigger they are, the harder they fall. And *he's* so big that when he comes down the crash is awful.'

'The young American in love,' Stagg grinned.

'Let's cut off his left ear like Van Gogh,' Slingsby suggested, 'and send it to her with the legend "Faithful unto Death" written in blood on the box.'

It seemed only fair to be helpful. 'Her name's Olga,' I said.

Tucker's eyes shone. 'How do you know?'

'You don't suppose it's tattooed on her forehead, do you? She told me.'

'She was French, Ah think,' Munro put in help-fully. 'She seemed tae understan' a wee bit o' what Ah was sayin'.'

I grinned. 'She's Russian,' I said. 'She's Puddy's sister. And she speaks excellent English. But not *your* English, you damned heathen. She thought you were a Hungarian.'

There was a yell of laughter from the rest of the flight and for the rest of the day Slingsby kept going up to Munro to ask if he'd like to dance a czardas or a mazurka, while Jasper inquired if he knew Lizst.

His only reply was to scowl and shout furiously. 'Och, awa' wi' ye!' to which Slingsby commented: 'Speaking Magyar, I think. Or it could be Armenian or Serbo-Croat.'

The following morning, Sykes returned from Ekat with orders. 'Bit of a flap on,' he said. 'Concentrations of Bolshevik troops are building up along the railway towards Slavyansk. The DH9s are loading up with 112-pound bombs to try to break them up. We'll be going along as protection.'

As we lifted off the ground, I noticed with sudden alarm a black Albatros coming down on the rear of the flight and was just about to signal a break when it banked into position so that I saw the red, white and black rondels on its wings and realized it was Pudhovkhin.

He slipped alongside me and waved, grinning all over his face, but it was still a little unnerving to see that machine right by my elbow. Too many times I'd been only too glad to get out of their way, because they'd terrified me more than once – especially when I'd been flying Pups, which were no match for them. With their shark noses, spade tails and souped-up engines, they'd been formidable opponents.

We found the Bolshevik troops just north of a village called Lovny. They were cavalry and there seemed to be hundreds of them, fur-capped men on shaggy ponies, their bodies strung about with ammunition belts. They obviously didn't know how to react to aeroplanes, however, and remained in a solid bunch, a great blob of humanity on the empty steppe, swarming across the railway line. As the DH9s approached, white faces turned up to watch and the next moment the bombs were whistling down among them. Puffs of smoke and flashes of flame broke out among them with those peculiar little shock waves that always surround an explosion, as though the blast was driving away all the air from the immediate vicinity. Even with the bombs dropping among them, the horsemen still didn't seem to catch on to the idea of scattering and just waited dumbly for the next lot of aeroplanes to come over.

We were circling above the bombers when I spotted three or four black dots moving up to us from the north and almost immediately recognized a mixed patrol of Red aeroplanes. There was a Spad, a Nieuport, a Fokker triplane and two Albatroses and I decided it was going to be tricky. In a fight you didn't wait to identify wing markings but fired automatically when a recognizable shape came into your sights, and with Pudhovkhin floating around in that black Albatros of his and the enemy in French machines we were going to have to be careful.

The Russians weren't very good and I saw Sykes chasing the Spad to the north until he seemed to realize his danger, let it go and turned south again. Pudhovkhin was better than I'd expected and he drove down one of the Albatroses. Its pilot didn't seem to know what to do and just went lower and lower with Pudhovkhin hovering above and behind his tail, squirting short bursts at him until, in what looked to me like a panicky attempt to land, the Bolshevik pilot touched his wheels down to the ground and managed to crash.

There was a puff of dust and pieces of aeroplane flew off, then the tail came up and it stood on its nose. Watching, I saw the pilot climb out and start running towards the north where the horsemen were, but Pudhovkhin had turned and was flying over the crashed machine about thirty feet up from the ground. Lines of tracer caught up with the running Russian and he went over like a shot rabbit and lay still. Even now, Pudhovkhin banked and came round again and I saw the spurts of dust lifting round the body as he emptied his guns into it before returning south.

When we got back, Sykes went for him in a fury. He wasn't playing according to the rules we'd learned in France. Although some people took the view that an enemy pilot who escaped was fair game because he could well be in the air again the following day shooting at your friends, most of us had never gone along with the idea and generally treated an enemy pilot who'd survived simply as a fellow airman. Pudhovkhin's attitude was somewhat different. He was a refined man who'd served in one of the Tsar's crack cavalry regiments before joining the Imperial Air Force but he had no intention of apologizing.

'We are proud and grateful to have you fighting with us, Sir Colonel,' he said to Sykes. 'But you do not understand the circumstances from Russian point of view. If I fall into hands of Bolsheviks I should be *tortured* – not just killed.'

He described how naval officers of the Black Sea Fleet had been massacred by their men. They had been given the choice of dying 'hot' or dying 'cold'. If they chose hot, they were tied to planks and fed inch by inch into the ship's furnaces. If they chose cold, they had iron bars tied to their feet and were dropped into the sea.

'Every man among us has had atrocities perpetrated against our families,' he said. 'Some of my own family were caught and I have not heard from them since. I try not to think what happened to them. This is a personal question between ourselves and the Bolsheviks.'

Sykes' background and ancestry were quite as select as Pudhovkhin's and it took a lot to disconcert him, but for once he was at a loss for words.

'Wonder if you can blame them,' he said thoughtfully as Pudhovkhin disappeared.

He shrugged off his flying coat. 'I know the monarchy was weak,' he went on, half to himself. 'I know that the nobility was a privileged and thin-blooded lot and that the whole country was riddled with graft, with a corrupt Church, a secret police and Siberia always in the background. I also know that in its last days the monarchy was run by an unscrupulous monk chap called Rasputin and that he possessed an extraordinary power over the Empress and she in her turn influenced every decision the Tsar made. All the same—' he peeled off his helmet and ran a hand through his flattened hair '—it doesn't help you much to understand it, does it, Brat, because the White Army's not just made up of the nobility. A lot of them are officers who took an oath to serve the Tsar, or professional classes who don't like being pushed around by a lot of jolly old demagogues.' He managed a wry smile and set off for the mess car. 'Nothin' quite so nasty as a civil war,' he ended. 'Read that somewhere. Think there must be some truth in it.'

As I followed him, wiping at the oily muck on my face that had been sprayed out by the Camel, I had a chilly feeling that he was right and we were fighting in the sort of campaign that was going to grow a whole lot worse.

—

Sykes stayed with us for a few days, but he didn't get in much flying and eventually he was called down to Ekat again. Almost immediately, he sent news that General Holman, the head of the British Mission in South Russia, was going to the Front on a tour of inspection and that we were to keep an eye on his train. Then a wire came to say I had to fly down to meet the general at Taganrog and get his itinerary.

I was told I could land on the racecourse but, to my surprise, there was a meeting on and everything stopped while I landed. As I climbed down, I was surrounded by officers in smart uniforms and chattering women in bright spring clothes, and it seemed typical of their attitude that they could happily attend a race meeting while their country was falling apart round their ears.

I got someone to guard the machine and, borrowing a car and a chauffeur, found Holman's train waiting in a siding just to the north of the city. It consisted of several carriages pulled by a ninety-ton monster of an engine decorated in red and black and liberally sprinkled with flags. There were more flags on the front and rear of the train and the corners of each carriage. Holman was a giant of a man with white hair and a ready smile and it was clear that, despite the fact that he spoke Russian well and understood the Russians, he didn't think much of the White organization.

'Too much of the equipment sent out from the United Kingdom's been finding its way to civilian homes,' he said. 'I suppose there's a good reason for it, because a lot of them are half-clothed and dreading the winter, and a lot of them are hungry and penniless, but that isn't why it was sent out and I'm going to the Front myself to see what's happening.'

He gave me tea and showed me round the train, which also included box cars for horses and a couple of flat cars to carry a motor car.

'I don't know whether I shall be operating by motor or train or on horseback,' he pointed out, 'so I have to be prepared for all emergencies.' He smiled. 'I'm not sure that I need an air escort, anyway,' he ended, 'but the authorities insist that it would be a disaster to their cause if I were killed or captured and I suppose they're right.'

There was a hospital train nearby that had a familiar look about it and I thought I'd pay a call.

It was packed with wounded men lying in double bunks against both walls, with only a narrow passageway between them for the hospital staff. These seemed to be the bad cases and most of them were half-unconscious, though one or two moaned and I saw one weeping silently into his hands. The doctor was a young Jew called Abramov, plump and smiling, with a pair of pince-nez'on a large bony nose. He spoke French and we conversed easily as he showed me through the hospital cars. They were all depressingly the same, and on the end was a typhus ward, consisting of an isolated car.

'There is so much dirt, you see,' he said. 'And when they are bitten by fleas which have been on the bodies of men who have had typhus, so it spreads. If we don't contain it, it could become a plague. Come, you must have a glass of tea.'

It wasn't tea I was wanting but it seemed good manners. He showed me how to drink it Russian fashion with a cube of sugar between my teeth and after a couple of tries I got the hang of it.

'I'm looking for a nurse,' I said hesitantly. 'Perhaps you know her. Her name's Pudhovkhina.'

He smiled immediately. 'But of course,' he said. 'Everybody looks for Olga Ivanovna.'

'Oh? Why?'

He lifted his hands in an expressive gesture. 'Because she is beautiful. And because she is very young and romantic and has such a sweet nature.'

She hadn't seemed very sweet when she'd walked out on me at the dance and Abramov listened to the story, smiling all the time in his gentle way.

'She has much tragedy, that one,' he said. 'Her father was murdered by his own troops and her mother and her little sister simply disappeared. No one knows what happened to them. There is now only Olga Ivanovna and her brother.' He sighed. 'And perhaps she is tired. She works tremendously long hours.'

He smiled apologetically. 'There are nurses and nurses, you see. Some of them are just ladies who are following their menfolk around and have no qualifications at all, so they are of little use. We have none of these with us. Ours are the other kind, who have worked in hospitals during the war and are now invaluable because of their skill. Since there aren't many of them, they are *all* overworked.'

He lit a long black cigarette which he held in his fingers in the curious back-to-front manner the Russians affected.

'We owe our nurses so much, Sir Major,' he went on enthusiastically. 'Many of them had never done a day's work before the war but now they shame us with their devotion. They endure the same hardships as anyone and are always short of warm clothes and the ordinary comforts of life.' He sighed. 'Sometimes I think there are many officers who might well profit by their example.' He paused and smiled. 'But I am sure you have not come to hear me talk. What do you want with Olga Ivanovna?'

I explained my wish to apologize and he rose, smiling. 'I'll find her,' he said, 'and send her to you.'

A few minutes later Olga herself appeared. She was wearing the black hood all Russian nurses wore and she was blushing. Her face was stiff but I had a suspicion that she wasn't really as angry as she pretended to be.

I said my piece and apologized humbly for any offence I'd given. To my surprise, she suddenly smiled.

'I think I am too angry,' she said. 'But I am pleased you have come to apologize. We must have a "five o'clock" and you must drink some Russian tea.'

I tried to explain that I'd just had some but she wouldn't listen and a fresh tray was brought in.

'You must learn to drink it Russian fashion,' she said.

'I can,' I said.

'You have learned?'

'One of our Russian officers taught me,' I lied.

She was only eighteen but she'd probably seen more of life and tragedy than most people do in a lifetime.

'Sometimes,' she said, with the same sad smile her brother had, 'it is hard not to think of the old days – the Mariinsky Theatre, Chaliapin at the Opera, matinées at the Dvorianskoe Sobranie, bonbons from Elieseff's. It's all gone now. I was in Petrograd when the October revolution broke out. The hatred for us was unbelievable. I suppose as a class we deserved what happened.'

She sighed. 'We had such good friends, you see,' she went on. 'Kind friends. Gentle friends. And I often think how wonderful it will be when we are all together again.'

I said nothing because I had a feeling that a great deal of time – perhaps years, perhaps never – was going to elapse before her ideal of happiness was reached.

She'd started nursing while she was still only fifteen and had served for two years on the Austrian Front. She had hated the Austrians but she loathed the Bolsheviks because the previous spring they'd appeared unexpectedly at Koryesevo where she'd been stationed and burned down the hospital with five hundred wounded men and all the medical staff inside. She'd escaped only because she'd been given permission to visit her brother who was flying from an airfield twenty miles to the west.

Her face was taut and her eyes seemed enormous as she told me. Then she seemed to make an effort to thrust it into the background as I'd noticed so many of the White Russians did, as though they liked to remind themselves what they were up against then forget it quickly so they could live ordinary human lives. If they hadn't done this, I suppose, what most of them had seen or experienced would have transformed their whole existence.

'Perhaps next time we are near,' she said, 'you will manage to ask me to dance again.'

I flew back to Debaltsevo with Holman's itinerary and a letter from Charley which he'd passed on to me. 'I expect this will spread alarm and despondency across South Russia,' she wrote, 'but the parents have decided that they're going to Nice for the summer. *I'm* going because otherwise they'll lose their passports as usual, have their money stolen, and be rooked by French shysters from every corner of the Riviera. With the economic situation as it is and you fighting in Russia, I heartily disapprove, of course.'

The thought of Charley marshalling her spendthrift parents round the South of France in her firm no-nonsense way tickled me, because no one could ever be in any doubt about it when Charley disapproved. You could just about as easily remain ignorant of an escape of gas in the room.

'I think they're still not used to the idea,' she continued, 'that I've set my heart on a funny-looking little airman called Martin Falconer whose only qualification, as far as I can see, is that he happens to have kindly thoughts about me, and they're obviously hoping I'll meet a French count or one of those awful British "weeds" who make a habit of spending the summer in the South of France. I'd much rather have my fierce old Martin.'

Me? Fierce? It was a picture of myself that had never occurred to me before but then I remembered that there'd been times in the past when I'd discovered I could be bad-tempered that Sykes had called 'the fuss and feathers of a budding senior officer'.

I wrote back at once, a long screed in which I tried to tell her something about the situation around me. To me, too, it seemed crazy that one half of the world could live in comfort and luxury while the other half lived in squalor and misery and revolution. To me then it seemed that Great Britain, America and France and a few others could well have got together and pulled out a few stops on behalf of those who had nothing. It was expecting too much, of course, because that was never how things worked.

I tried also to tell her about Olga, dwelling not on her charm but on the horrors she'd experienced.

I didn't think there'd be any jealousy from Charley because she wasn't made that way but I played safe just the same and described the war rather than the party where we'd met.

The following morning we received a signal from Sykes in Ekat to the effect that Holman's train had left and was already heading north. As it happened, the Reds didn't seem to be the slightest bit interested in Holman but we broke up with our machine-guns a bunch of Red cavalry we saw about twenty miles east of the railway line and when a flight of mixed Spads and Nieuports came up to have a look at us we drove them off without difficulty. As they dived away to the north, I was just drawing breath and thinking what a nice easy little skirmish it had been when I saw tracers and something shot past my wingtip. It was a Fokker triplane painted all white with the red stars of the Bolsheviks standing out on the wings like great splashes of blood.

One of the White Russian Moranes was just breaking up a hundred yards away. I saw the flying wires flapping wildly, then one of the wings seemed to detach itself as if it had been chopped off with an axe, and floated away behind the machine as it began to go down in a flat spin, the sound wing carrying the fuselage round and round the broken one. Then the good wing came off, too, the nose dipped and the fuselage hurtled towards the earth like a spent rocket, the tail wagging with the speed of its descent.

By this time both flights had scattered and a whirling dogfight was taking place. My friend in the white Fokker triplane had gone up like a lift, standing on his tail and climbing like a hawk, all three sets of wings dragging him up. Then he dropped his nose and came down on us again, and I saw Munro and Tommy Tucker go for him. He was too clever for them by a long way, though, and they almost collided as he slipped between them so that I wondered if he was some German flier from the Western Front with a couple of years of war flying experience behind him, who'd joined the Reds as a mercenary or because he didn't know what to do with the peace. We'd heard of Americans and polit-ically motivated Canadians, Australians, and French who believed in the Reds' Brave New World.

I went after the white triplane with the engine screaming, but he was clever enough to slip away again, and then a drab khaki-coloured machine slipped in front of me and, as I went after that one instead, I saw it was a Fokker DVII.

This altered things considerably because the coffin-like DVII with its comma tail was one of the best machines that had ever been built and they'd frightened me silly all too often in France. They had BMW six-cylinder engines and welded-tubing fuselages and, because the wings were in one piece with the spars running from end to end, they were as strong as mules and had no bad habits. If the Reds had got hold of a few of those, we were likely to be up against tougher opposition.

I stood the Camel on a wingtip and went after it, but it dived away and I found myself face to face with the white triplane again. As I pressed the trigger button, I heard a bullet clang on the engine cowling, then splinters leapt from the centre section struts and little flags of fabric started flapping on my wings.

We were still heading for each other at a combined speed of over two hundred miles an hour and if one of us didn't pull aside soon, there wasn't going to be much left of either of us. But I'd learned long ago that the man who lost his nerve first in a face-to-face encounter was usually a dead duck and, knowing how well triplanes climbed, I suspected that if the other pilot did break away, he'd go above me.

Sure enough, just when I thought we were going to crash, the white machine lifted like a Venetian blind going up, but I was ready and as it went I pulled back on the stick a fraction and raked the square belly from nose to stern. Standing the Camel on its wingtip again, I hurtled round at full speed, to find myself flying through fragments of white wood and fabric. An aileron floating through the air came whipping back past me, then I saw the wreckage of a top wing, still with the red splash of colour on the canvas, float by. As I pulled out of the turn, the white fuselage passed underneath and I watched it crash into a small fir forest in a flare of flame and smoke.

When we got back we counted noses. We'd lost nobody, but the brown Fokker DVII had put bullets through Tucker's tail and the Russian squadron had lost four of their Moranes. It seemed to knock the stuffing out of them, and I could hardly blame them because you couldn't tackle DVIIs with obsolete Moranes.

With the Russian squadron's losses, there was gloom about the squadron trains that night which was not made better by the news that the French had evacuated Sebastopol in the Crimea. They had even scuttled several submarines and small ships and got out with the same hurry they'd shown at Odessa, and Pudhovkhin and the other Russians were walking about with long faces.

Things suddenly didn't look very encouraging, especially as it seemed the Bolsheviks had also grabbed power in Hungary to the south. All those toasts of '*Na Moskvu,*' 'To Moscow', that we'd heard when we'd first arrived seemed to have gone up into thin air, and, as a few of the temporary officers, who had never intended fighting anyway, managed to slip away and vanish southwards, there was a rash of desertions among their men. You could hardly blame them. They were underpaid and underfed and treated like dirt by their officers. Many times I'd seen them sitting in their cars as their soldiers pushed them free of the mud patches, none of them ever considering the possibility of getting out to make the load lighter.

Overnight everyone began to predict disaster and it seemed that we went from day to day expecting it. But, in May, with the steppes around us coming to life and the sky filled with larks' song and coveys of partridges bursting up out of the long grass, the pendulum swung violently back again. Wrangel had won a victory at a place with a name we couldn't pronounce and we began to hope that Denikin would launch major operations against Kharkov and Tsaritsyn. Almost immediately, a signal arrived that we were to leave Debaltsevo and take our trains over towards the Volga Front and operate alongside 47 Squadron from Beketofka. I was a bit afraid that I'd lose track of the hospital train because I was very anxious to make up for my rudeness with a party and another dance with Puddy's sister, but, as we left, a medical orderly arrived with a message to the effect that the hospital trains had been told to unload their wounded on to trains headed for Ekaterinodar and also head for the Volga.

Because of the Russian railway system, which was never very complex, we had to head back to Makeyevka, Taganrog and Rostov-on-Don and down to Tikoretskaya, then head north again further east towards Tsaritsyn. It was a slow journey because half of Russia seemed to be on the move now that the weather was warm and dry, and the refugee trains seemed to have as many people on the outside as they had inside, whole families clinging to roofs, running boards and buffers. The steppes were lovely, a little like Salisbury Plain and full of birds' songs. They were covered with long grass with, here and there, masses of wild blooms, patches of golden sunflowers or acres of blue and pink, so that our nostrils were filled with perfume. But there was no made road of any kind and never a soul in sight.

Occasionally, we passed through a village that had been raided by Red cavalry and there were a few holes where shells had fallen, a few charred houses, dead chickens and even occasional dead horses still in the shafts of their carts, and from time to time we passed White Army troops alongside their encampments. They were still shockingly badly equipped. Some of them had no boots and I saw hardly any machine-guns. Their faces, covered with dust, were blank and haggard and you could often see knees and elbows through their worn uniforms. Their shirts were discoloured and threadbare and many of the men lacked them altogether and wore only woollen vests, while others actually wore the spiked *pickelhaube* helmets left behind by the Germans in 1918.

When we arrived near Beketofka, 47 Squadron, several of whom I knew well, were crowing because they considered it had been their efforts that had brought about Wrangel's victory. There was a lot of confusion, however, because Wrangel had been down with typhus and Denikin had not had the courage to put any one White general under the command of any other so that they were all operating separately. Despite the poor organization and poor supplies, however, Wrangel had still managed, with the aid of Don, Circassian and Astrakhan Cossacks, to destroy the Tenth Red Army, and expected to be at the gates of Tsaritsyn in a matter of weeks.

To back him up, we were flung into the fray at once. On this Front the Bolshevik airmen seemed to be more lively and we'd been warned that they even had bombers. There seemed to be plenty of fighters, too, and we joined 47 Squadron in downing quite a few of them. Rhatanyi's White Russian DH9s were also busy with the A and B Flight machines and we were always having to rush to their assistance because, like the rest of the Whites, they were far too casual in their planning, and indifferent in the maintenance of their aeroplanes.

'Of course,' Pudhovkhin explained, 'among their men may be Bolshevik sympathizers who sabotage their aeroplanes. You should be glad that you have British mechanics.'

I tried to persuade him to take over a spare Camel in case one of the 47 Squadron pilots had a go at him by mistake, but he said he was used to the black Albatros and preferred something he knew to something he didn't.

'Russians are not mechanically minded,' he said. 'And perhaps I might do something silly and end up having to force-land in front of General Budenny's Red cavalry.' He gave a beaming smile. 'I would not like that.'

He was probably right and he was certainly better off than the other White Russians because constantly their engines let them down and their guns jammed, and they were irresponsible and casual to the point of madness.

'They couldn't hit a bull in a passage,' Slingsby observed cheerfully. 'Not even a big bull.'

'They're brave enough, of course,' Jasper said.

'Aye,' Munro agreed. '*Too* brave. They dinnae tak' care o' the details an' their machines are always disappearin' – lost or downed wi' engine failure.'

'And they can't keep a formation to save their lives,' Tucker added. 'So that they're never able to give each other any support whatsoever, when they're attacked.'

'This morn,' Munro said darkly, 'Ah had tae chivvy two of 'em back to the flock. Yesterday Ah had tae escort one home because he was lost.' He stared pointedly at me as if it were my fault. 'One o' these days Ah'll be doin' that when Ah ought tae be keepin' an eye on you or Slingsby or Tommy. An' next time one of 'em puts a burst intae ma tail in his panic when Ah'm tryin' tae do him a favour, Ah'll shoot him down.'

Despite the grumbles, the job we were there for had to be done. We went out again and again with them towards Tsaritsyn and, sure enough, one day we were caught. As soon as the first mixed bag of British, French and German machines came up at us, the Russian DH9s dropped their bombs as fast as they could and bolted for home, lumbering round in flat turns, as though their pilots were terrified of putting their machines into a bank – which a lot of them were! The bombs dropped in a solid shower on the edge of Tsaritsyn without doing much damage, then we realized the DH9s were all over the sky and the Red planes were pecking at them without interference. One of them went down in flames and I saw the observer jump out in a whirl of arms and legs, then, as we tried to get the rest of them into a bunch so we could shepherd them home, another flight of assorted fighters came down on us. Fortunately, 47 Squadron, escorting Russian DHs of their own, saw the fight from the other side of Tsaritsyn and came hurtling into the fray just as another bunch of Bolshevik scouts, led by our old friend the brown Fokker, who'd also changed Fronts, it seemed, arrived from the opposite direction. It was as big a dogfight as some I'd seen in France, with aeroplanes whirling all over the sky.

One of the DH9s I was edging to safety was clearly being manoeuvred by a panicking pilot and he allowed his machine to stall. As the nose dropped he was caught by the brown Fokker, and the nose didn't come up again so that the machine went into a screaming perpendicular dive, with pieces of the wing coming off all the way down, until it smashed into the River Volga. Then another one, trying to fly in formation, touched wings with a third, and fluttered away, its wings crumpled, and wobbled down until that, too, disappeared below us. I hoped to God it didn't land among the Bolshevik soldiers.

Munro was on the tail of a Spad and the Spad's tail was in ribbons, and I saw Tucker going round in a wild merry-go-round with a triplane. An Albatros appeared in my sights and I was just going to fire when I realized it was black and that it wore red, white and black rondels instead of red stars and was piloted by Puddy Pudhovkhin. I allowed him to slip away and instead took on another Albatros that was trying to get on his tail. The pilot flew straight into my stream of bullets, and the nose of his machine dipped and he went into a dive that grew steeper until the machine was beyond the vertical in an inverted loop. When the pilot fell out, I hoped he was dead, because he had a long way to go and, like the rest of us, had no parachute.

Then, within a second, the sky seemed to be empty. The DH9s were scurrying south in the loose bunch they liked to call a formation and 47 Squadron were grouping together a little to the east. The rest formed up on me and we headed for home. When we counted noses, we found that 47 Squadron had lost two DH9s and shot down two fighters, while we'd lost three DH9s, two of them through their own fault or inexperience, and shot down three fighters, so the scores were fairly even.

Tucker's machine had a few holes in it but he seemed to regard it as just part of the fun.

'I guess the other guy has more in his,' he laughed.

He was in high spirits because he hadn't seen enough of the war in France to be afraid. 'Rhatanyi says that Wrangel's Cossacks are forming up in front of Tsaritsyn,' he informed us. 'They're preparing to take the place,' he said, 'and it seems we prevented the Bolshies occupying positions opposite them. Maybe it was worth all those lives.'

Munro gave him a long slow look. He looked exhausted by the fight and I wondered suddenly if he'd been wise to come to Russia at all so soon after that appalling accident in France that had chopped him up so badly.

'Ma sweet American Sunny Jim,' he said sadly. 'All'll tell ye a secret. Ah learned it during four years o' fightin' in France: it's *never* worth it.'

Chapter 4

Standing alongside the train near the railway track, we could see the flickering lights on the horizon where Wrangel's forces were hammering at Tsaritsyn. For days, with few supplies, his troops had marched across several hundred kilometres of barren steppes, smashing every Red strongpoint they'd met. Although it was mid-May now, the nights were still quite cold and damp with a great deal of wet mist, and he had had scores of cases of pneumonia.

Despite his appeals for help, Denikin, keen to be the first man to Moscow, was still pressing on the Kharkov Front and was ignoring him, and Wrangel himself, despite a recent attack of typhus, had had to make most of the journey to Tsaritsyn on horseback. When his motor vehicles wore out their tyres, he wound ropes round the wheels and continued on those.

Our trains were moving up just behind him, and there were several Kalmuk cavalrymen from his staff who kept dropping in for meals. Although they were Don Cossacks they were of Mongol appearance and were Buddhists. They were fiercely anti-Bolshevik and excellent fighters, but their men occasionally got out of hand and when they did they were incredibly cruel. When we finally reached Tsaritsyn and our train came up behind them, they returned our hospitality under the green and yellow crescented flag that flew over their mess.

The advance, which had been doing so well, had come to a stop again. Despite the telegrams that had been sent to Denikin asking for men and equipment, none arrived and it was obvious that there was a great deal of resentment against the commander-in-chief among Wrangel's troops.

'It is because fresh Bolshevik units are moving into Tsaritsyn from the north,' Pudhovkhin explained. 'If Wrangel leaves his attack too long, it will be disaster.'

'An' if he throws it in the noo it might *also* be a disaster,' Munro observed.

We'd done our share, ground-strafing as we'd learned to do so successfully in France against the retreating Germans in 1918. 47 Squadron, operating from Beketofka, were also doing their stuff, but the Reds had seemed to sense that Wrangel was running short of supplies and had counter-attacked to drive him back to the Tchervlennia River, and we and 47 Squadron were standing by once more for orders to pull out to the south.

'Wrangel cannae get his supplies because Denikin's keepin' 'em for his own advance along the Don,' Munro growled. 'He wants tae be in Moscow by October an' he just isnae interested in *us*.'

While we were eating our evening meal, the temperature dropped and the mist thickened until it was almost like a fog, clinging, wet and grey, leaving us in a curious isolation with our train. It was a strange feeling to listen to the mutter of guns and small arms to the north, aware that all round us there was nothing but the bare steppe. It left a nasty uneasy chill down your back, because Bolshevik patrols liked to take advantage of darkness and mist and fall on White outposts with their own particular brand of ferocity.

'47 Squadron was up taeday,' Munro was saying. 'Ah haird they were sent oot tae find Budenny an' the Red cavalry.'

'Any casualties?' Tucker asked and I knew he was wondering if he could find an excuse to go and look for Train Number 643.

'None Ah haird of,' Munro said. 'But mebbe the Reds had a few.'

While we were talking, we heard the sound of a car engine outside and crowded on to the platform at the end of the mess Pullman to see what was happening. A car came bouncing across the steppe towards the railway line, its lights dim yellow glows through the mist. Inside it was one of Wrangel's Caucasian officers with Marcus Kinkead, who was running 47 Squadron's Camels.

'Wrangel's going in tomorrow,' he announced. 'He got his reinforcements after all – an infantry division and five batteries of artillery. He's decided to take a chance, and it's up to you. We caught Budenny this morning, fifteen miles north of the city and tore lumps out of his cavalry. General Shkura's Cossacks say there were around eight hundred dead.'

'How about wounded?' Tucker asked.

Kinkead shook his head. 'When Shkura's Cossacks follow up,' he pointed out, 'there are *never* any wounded. Only dead.'

We'd heard of Shkura. His men were called the Wolves and a wolf's head was their badge. Their Cossack caps were made of shaggy wolf's fur instead of the usual astrakhan wool, and with a reputation for bloodthirstiness and pleasure in pillage, they had even been known to rob gatherings of White officers on the understanding that they needed money and the officers had it.

'We lost no one,' Kinkead went on, 'but some of the machines were pretty badly shot up. They had machine-guns and we'll need a day or so for repairs. It seems to be up to you.'

–

Not long after dawn the following day we heard renewed firing and the sound of horses nearby, and saw columns of horsemen moving north to the creak of leather and jingle of equipment. An hour later we were flying low over Wrangel's tanks, armoured cars and cavalry as they closed in on Tsaritsyn.

I could see the artillery firing and groups of men with unfurled banners drawn up in lines and columns. Among them were bands and buglers and standards floating on the breeze. Occasionally the sun caught the flash of swords as the men began to move forward in a cloud of dust. War must have been like this in the days before the petrol engine, I thought, and then it dawned on me I was looking down on a battle much as Napoleon must have seen it, when men in gorgeous uniforms charged with snapping banners over green meadows against enemy batteries.

Behind the first troops, country carts were moving up with more batteries of guns. A shell tossed up dirt near them, followed by another and another and a conference of senior officers split up hurriedly as the enemy missiles found them. Then two companies of horsemen trotted forward with carts containing machine-guns and began to dash towards the city in fine style, the carts bouncing over the folds of the ground at top speed and flinging up clouds of dust. A few men were hit, two horses went down and one of the carts overturned.

My compass was acting strangely and was quite unreliable, but with the others around and plenty of landmarks I wasn't worried. Ahead I could see the Bolshevik barbed wire being smashed down by the tanks and saw a division of Kuban Cossacks forming for a charge. The Kubans were quite different from the men of the Don – dark unshaven men who looked like Afghans and wore the long black-waisted coat which was peculiar to their area, together with an array of black and silver inlaid daggers, swords, old-fashioned pistols, and decorative cartridges in a line across the chest. Their patois was barely understandable, and unlike the Don Cossacks, who were lancers, they were swordsmen.

As I banked over the battlefield, I could see a great phalanx of them on the plain just to the south of the city. Then I saw a whole line of guns in a stand of trees beyond the smashed wire and what looked like machine-guns on either side of the short valley that led down to them. The Cossacks were heading into a perfect Balaclava situation, facing down a valley to charge guns, with more guns on either side of them hidden by a dip in the ground. As we circled over them, I could even see the gun teams waiting beyond the trees, lines of horses with limbers and ammunition waggons, and more carts in the dip near the nests of machine-guns.

The Cossacks began to edge forward, their vedettes already under long-range fire. Then Red cavalry appeared behind the guns in support. They were followed by carts and were just beginning to cross a long wooden bridge of boats and trestles across a river.

I waggled my wings and pointed and the whole crowd of us, me in front with Munro and Jasper on one side and Slingsby and Tucker on the other, went down in a shallow dive. The sound of the wind through the wires became a howl and, as the seconds passed, I saw the guns growing larger and larger in my sights. As the twin Vickers began to rattle and shake, khaki-clad men jumped up and white faces turned in our direction. Figures fell and spurts of dust sprang from the earth around the field guns. Coming on them from the rear, we had found them entirely unprepared and, as we banked away, I saw the machine-gunners on either side of the valley struggling to bring their weapons to bear. We tore into them before they could shift position and I saw them packing up and starting to leave, men running with their heavy weapons in their arms towards the waiting carts. We caught them before they reached them and they went down in a heap among the jumping dust.

Then we attacked the carts. I hated shooting horses, because it seemed to me that while men had some sort of choice in war, horses didn't, but there was no option. Horses represented transport and if the guns were moved they could be brought into action again, while the Cossacks, now forming into line for their advance, could capture or destroy the lot if we could stop them being moved. The horses reared and plunged, dropping in kicking heaps, and though I hated the butchery, not one of the machine-guns got away and I could see the Cossacks now beginning to move forward for their charge across the wire.

The Red cavalrymen were still crossing the wooden bridge in a long file, hurrying now, as though they'd realized what was happening in front of them, and we caught them there, where they couldn't escape. Men and horses crashed into the river and I could see the splashes of bullets pursuing them along the surface of the water. A few galloped ahead, trying to reach the other side, but a horse slipped and fell and, as they began to bunch, I saw the frail structure collapse, throwing them into the water. The rest tried to turn and make their way back but the other end had been blocked by fallen horses and stalled carts and all they could do was spur their mounts into the river and try to escape by swimming.

There were still the field guns at the end of the valley in the trees but they weren't waiting for the arrival of the Cossacks. The gunners were already wheeling the teams of horses round and backing them up to the tails of the guns, and we were on them while they were still trying to hitch the weapons to the limbers. As we lifted away at last with empty guns I saw that the bridge of boats and trestles was burning, the smoke hanging low over the water in the reeds. At the far end was a tangle of men and animals and a horse was struggling to rise in the harness that held it to its dead companions, while another, its coat gleaming with water, lay in the shallows, its legs in the air.

Then, quite plainly, I saw the officer in command of the Cossacks sitting his horse near a farm wave his sword. One or two of the retreating guns stopped long enough to open fire and the Cossacks wavered as the shells fell among them. A horse dropped with kicking legs, then I saw the officers set about their men with the flat of their swords. Sickle-like sabres flashed in the sun and the pace of the horses changed to a canter and they swept onwards to join other formations coming in from the flanks. God only knew what sort of slaughter went on down there but not a single gun escaped.

'Talk about alarm and despondency,' Slingsby chirruped as we landed. 'We had 'em running about like hens in hysterics.'

Three days later Wrangel had control of Tsaritsyn and long lines of men, stripped of their weapons and often of their clothes and boots, were heading south. Their choice was either to join the Whites or be murdered, a policy I'd always considered pretty dangerous because at the next reversal of fortune they'd only change sides again.

There seemed little to stop Wrangel now and by 19 May the Reds were fleeing north of the Volga, and forty thousand prisoners and a mountain of supplies had been captured. I'd been looking forward to seeing inside a civilized town again after so long living in the steppes on the train, but we were ordered to see the Reds off and, instead of visiting Tsaritsyn, spent our time chasing them up the west bank of the Volga.

Both squadrons were on the job, followed up by the Russian and British DH9s. Miles north of Tsaritsyn we hammered at them with machine-guns and bombs, the idea being to stop them reforming into cohesive units – to keep them on the run, following Napoleon's old maxim of not halting after a victory until resistance began to form.

For two days we strafed groups of horsemen, waggons, lorries and men as they streamed north, then on the evening of the 21st, with mist already beginning to form in the folds of the ground and our guns and tanks empty, we ran into a beautifully laid trap. We'd been strafing small groups of horsemen and carts for some time when we saw a long column of waggons and swung towards them. They'd grown used to the strafing by this time, however, and they'd prepared a reception for us. As we poured down out of the sky, I saw canvas covers dragged clear and found myself staring into the muzzles of a whole battery of machine-guns. It was clearly time we got out.

I yanked at the stick and waved my arm, pointing upwards. As I lifted away, the others followed me, and, glancing over the side of the cockpit, I could see the machine-guns moving round with us as we climbed. As we swung south, we were followed by a hail of bullets and I saw little flags of fabric start to flap on the lower wing. Then I realized that Munro, who'd been on my right, had sagged out of sight and I saw him well below me, obviously in trouble. As I watched, he waved, and I realized he was going to have to land.

I thought of the number of times he'd sat on my tail in France keeping off the Germans, and the number of times I'd done the same for him, and with the Red cavalry only a mile or so away and able to see everything that was happening across the flat expanse of the steppes, I watched his wheels touch. There was a puff of dust, then the machine rolled to a stop.

I knew the Red cavalry must have seen him come down and that within a matter of minutes there'd be a strong patrol galloping forward to take him prisoner. A shot-down British airman, whether dead or alive, was good propaganda and they'd make a lot of it, and without hesitation, I waved to Slingsby to take over the flight and side-slipped down to where Munro was already climbing out of his machine. Rumbling to a stop alongside him, I saw him struggling to set fire to the Camel. There was a woof as the petrol went up and the wings immediately began to sag in the flames, then he hobbled towards me, looking scared but trying to grin.

'Severed a petrol feed,' he said. 'No' a chance tae repair it.'

I jerked a hand behind me. Small figures on horseback were already appearing on the horizon. Slingsby and the others had swung back to cover us but, as they dived on the horsemen, there were no more than a few bursts, then nothing more. Although they continued to dive, it didn't take long for the Bolsheviks to catch on to the fact that their guns were empty and, as they were obliged to swing round and head for home, short of petrol, the horsemen began to group together and press forward again.

Slingsby roared over us, the engine drowning my shouts with that peculiar crackling hiss a Camel made, and I could see the spray of castor oil it threw out forming a rainbow against the sky. He waved and pointed and I assumed he was trying to indicate that he was going to fetch help, but I knew that any help he could get was going to be too late and that, dud compass or no dud compass, the only person who could save Munro was me.

'For God's sake,' I said. 'Get aboard!'

'Where, mon, for God's sake?' Munro panted. 'A Camel's no' built for two.'

With his crippled legs, I knew he'd never be able to cram himself into the only place there was for a passenger in a Camel – above the guns – so I climbed out and signed to him to take over.

'You fly it,' I yelled and, as he dragged himself on to the fuselage, I jammed myself between the centre section struts. He didn't argue and slid into the cockpit and, without any further words, shoved the throttle wide open. The propeller was only about a couple of feet from my nose and the blast of air from it almost tore the clothes off me. I just hoped that Munro was as good a pilot as I thought he was.

The machine staggered off rather than took off, with Munro craning his head out of the side of the cockpit in an endeavour to see round me.

'I seem to make a habit of this sort of thing,' I yelled at him. 'I did it once before in France with Sykes.'

His smile was twisted and hurried as he concentrated. 'Ye're no' very big, Brat,' he yelled back. 'But Ah wish ye were a hell o' a sight smaller.'

We crabbed along about a hundred feet above the ground, with me yelling all the time – 'Keep it going! For God's sake, keep it going!'

He was having difficulty because the Camel was normally tail-heavy and now it was nose-heavy, and it behaved even worse that way. The Red cavalry patrol was a couple of miles behind us now, still following, but we were making progress and drawing further away from them all the time. The machine staggered on, wobbling rather than flying through the air, then I noticed that the mist which had been filling the valleys had grown thicker and was spreading across the plain. I turned my head and saw a thick swathe of it between us and the Reds, but I decided that, with neither of us able to see anything, and the compass useless, it seemed a good idea to go lower in the hope of picking up a landmark.

I pointed downwards and Munro nodded but, as he began to lower the machine into the mist, it was our bad luck that what was perhaps the only tree in that whole vast area of the steppe was in our way and Munro couldn't see it because I was bang in his line of vision. Out of the corner of my eye, I saw a roofless house and a broken fence, then a group of flattened trees, and at the end of the line, one of them standing up straight and stiff as a church spire.

'Climb!' I screamed as I saw it coming through the mist at me.

Munro yanked at the joystick and the Camel laboured up, but the wheels caught in the top branches and, as it nosed over, I felt the tree bending like a bow. Why I wasn't flung into the propeller I can't imagine, but as we hit the ground I saw it fly to pieces and heard the sound of shattering wood and tearing fabric, with the clattering of broken flying wires and a last agonized scream from the engine before it stopped, then I was sliding along the ground still jammed between the centre section struts. I seemed to go on for miles, still jammed between the fuselage and the top wing, then the wing fell off and I was ejected like a pip from an orange and sailed through the air to land on my back in a puff of dust.

For a moment I lay there, staring up into the gathering mist, then the stars stopped flashing and the earth stopped going round and I sat up.

Immediately, I realized that the mist had thickened sufficiently to hide us from the Reds and thanked Heaven for the small mercy of it. Munro was also sitting up. By a miracle neither of us seemed to be much hurt, but we were stuck out on the wide steppe about twenty miles north of Tsaritsyn with the Red cavalry not far away in the mist and, having heard the crash as they must have, probably heading at full speed in our direction at that very moment.

'I should think you managed to hit the only tree for miles around,' I said.

Munro shook his head to get his senses back. 'Wi' yon body o' yours right in front o' ma een, it's no' very surprisin'.' He turned and looked round him. 'What do we do the noo?'

The Camel seemed to have been spread over a distance of about thirty yards and it seemed a miracle that we were alive, let alone without anything broken.

'You all right?' I asked.

'Apart from a lump on ma heid as big as an eigg an' the fact that we're miles from onywhere an' I ha'e no' sticks tae walk wi', aye. You?'

There was a cut on my head that was leaking blood into my eye but it didn't seem very bad. 'Think we can get back to Tsaritsyn?' I asked.

Munro shook his head. '*You* might, Brat. Ah cannae.'

Knowing the damage he'd done to his legs long before I ever met him, I saw we had a problem.

'If only we could get a horse,' I said.

'From where? The Reds are over yonder.'

He offered me a cigarette as we wondered what to do. I was no smoker as a rule but just then it went a long way to steady my nerves.

'I could walk and try to bring help, Jock,' I said.

'Ah reckon yon's the only option we've got,' he agreed.

'Stay near the machine. We can get a DH9 down in the morning as soon as it's daylight. We know roughly where you are.'

'The Red Army's stopped retreating, ye'll have noticed,' he said, jerking a thumb to the north. 'That's why they had yon machine-guns waitin' for us. Tomorrow they'll start edging forward again so ye'd better mak' sure yon Nine's up above me *before* daylight.'

The matter was taken out of our hands, however. I'd noticed uneasily there was fresh manure in the grass nearby and, remembering flying over scattered groups of cavalry, I was just wondering if there were more of them near us when I spotted a figure looming up through the mist a few yards away.

'Quiet!'

Munro was just complaining about the fact that there were no hedges on the steppes from which to break a stick to help him walk and, as he stopped, you could almost cut the silence with a knife. The weather had deteriorated rapidly since we'd hit the ground and there was rain in the mist now. We peered through it anxiously at the motionless shape, then Munro jerked a hand and I saw another shape and then another, and then more and I realized they were all round us, large in the poor light, rifles and shaggy caps quite clear.

'We'd better separate, Jock,' I whispered. 'One of us might make it.'

'See an' find Barbara for me, then, and tell her what happened. She's been writin' lately tae say she's back in England and where have Ah got tae?'

'I've got to get out first,' I said, because I'd noticed that the men on horseback were moving closer.

Then a voice came through the mist, rough and heavy. '*Anglichanie!*'

'Lie down, Jock,' I said. 'They might just miss us.'

'*Anglichanie!*' The voice came again. 'However! Good morning!'

We were just wondering which way to run because the shaggy-capped figures were very close now, when the voice called again. '*Bozhe Tsarya khrani!* God – save – the – King.'

Then I remembered that the Red cavalry we'd been shooting at for days hadn't worn fur caps but khaki affairs with ear flaps, coming to a point at the top.

'It's not the Reds,' I said. 'It's Shkura's lot!'

We started to yell and immediately we seemed to be surrounded by horsemen with fierce eyes and grinning mouths beneath the shaggy fur. They seemed to be weighed down with weapons and ammunition, and I was delighted to see that they had one or two riderless horses with them.

One of them edged forward. '*Zdravstvuite*,' he said. 'Hello – good morning. I am Captain Machikov. Of Shkura.'

'Ah'm pleased tae meet ye,' Munro said. 'Mon, am Ah pleased!'

Machikov grinned. 'You ride?' he said.

I could ride but I knew Munro couldn't because he was a city dweller and his injured legs would never hold him in the saddle, anyway. They hoisted him up, nevertheless, and pointed south.

'*Pozhaluista*. Please. We go.'

Swinging the horses' heads, we turned into the mist in a straggling line. They seemed to know their way, and Munro and I clung close to them in case we got lost again.

'Is *Bolsheviki* near,' Captain Machikov said quietly. 'Strong patrol. Perhaps hundreds.'

He lifted two fingers to indicate two hundred and I hoped they weren't as near as he seemed to think.

'They come back.' He pointed south. 'To Tsaritsyn. Is not finish, the battle.'

I gathered that in Tsaritsyn there were already fears that they were going to have a job hanging on to the city, but at that moment all I was interested in was getting into it, through it, and well out of it at the other side.

It grew dark and I began to doze in the saddle as we rode. Every now and then a man cantered up to Machikov, pointed and spoke softly to him and, judging by the way our route twisted and turned, I guessed we were picking our way between scattered groups of Reds.

We seemed to have been riding forever when I glanced at my watch and I saw by the luminous dial that it was four a.m. We'd been riding all night. As I looked up again, the horse I was riding cannoned into the one in front.

'*Bozhe moi!*' Machikov was peering through the mist. A horseman appeared, the animal's hooves thudding softly on the turf, and there was a short conversation in Russian.

'Is Reds.' Up went the two fingers again. 'Two *sotnia*.'

I knew that a *sotnia* was a detachment of about a hundred men and I hurriedly counted our party. With Munro and me there were thirty-five of us.

'*Dobrovolcheskaya armiya*,' Machikov said and made signs with his hands to tell me that the Red patrol had got between us and Wrangel's army.

Then he grinned. '*Nichevo*. Is nothing. We will attack. Like at Balaclava the English. Very famous.'

'Oh, ma God,' Munro said. 'We're going to do a Light Brigade!'

'We save you,' Machikov said. '*Daite nam viski.* You give us whisky.'

I promised him all the whisky he could drink. '*Prazdnik*,' I said. 'Big party.'

He grinned and nodded, then he looked at Munro's clumsy seat. 'Is not good, that one,' he said, and before Munro knew what was happening, he was surrounded by dismounted men who were strapping him to the horse with belts and ropes.

'So not fall,' Machikov explained. It seemed there was going to be a little wild riding ahead and they were making sure Munro didn't slide off.

Machikov handed me a sabre. 'For *Bolsheviki*,' he said.

Its edge was like a razor and I decided that if I tried to use it I'd either cut off my own left arm or the horse's head and I pushed it back at him. 'Gun,' I said. 'Better.'

He grinned as I drew my revolver. Munro had dragged his own weapon out and was looking at me with the whites of his eyes showing like a startled foal's.

'Jock, old son,' I said, 'if we come through this lot, we'll be the only airmen in the world to have taken part in a cavalry charge.'

The Cossacks formed a rough line, with Munro and myself in the middle for safety.

'If trouble,' Machikov said, 'keep ride. On. To Tsaritsyn.' He pointed at Munro. 'Tell also.'

I turned in the saddle. 'He says that whatever happens we've to keep riding.'

Munro looked worried. 'If Ah once start, mon,' he said, 'ye couldnae stop me if ye tried. Come tae that, neither could I.'

The line moved forward gently, then Machikov lifted his hand. '*Stoy!* Halt!'

He leaned towards me. 'Metres,' he said and held up his fingers. 'Two. *Bolsheviki.*'

Bolsheviks two yards away! It didn't make sense. Then I realized he was trying to tell me the Bolsheviks were two *hundred* yards away.

'*Khorosho!* Good! Stay with. Same me. We go now. However! Good morning.'

I looked at Munro. A big sergeant had moved alongside him to hem him in but he still looked terrified. I expect I looked much the same. I held the reins in my left hand and clutched the revolver in the other. Munro was taking no chances and had stuffed the revolver away again and was hanging on to the reins with *both* hands.

The line of horsemen began to move slowly forward, and hearing a metallic slithering noise, I realized that the long sabres had been drawn. The Cossacks were leaning forward over their horses' necks now, the weapons held stiffly in front of them.

To right and left of me I could see horses' heads moving up and down, and fierce faces under the shaggy caps. Then as the speed increased I was left a little behind so that now it was the rumps of the horses I could see going up and down. The swish and drumming of hooves through the thick grass sounded loud in the stillness and the mist, then I heard a shout just ahead somewhere in the darkness – '*Radi Boga!*' – and saw the glow of a fire.

In front of me men were running for their lives, their horses scattering, then the Cossacks were going flat out, with Munro and I trying desperately to keep up with them. A man with a rifle appeared alongside me, but before he could pull the trigger,

Machikov's razor-like sabre swept down. It clashed against the barrel of the rifle and slithered along it, so that I saw the rifleman's hands fly up into the air, still holding the weapon. Another man appeared on my right. He had a lance and was pointing it straight at my chest. Pushing the revolver forward, I fired and he disappeared with a yell, his face dissolving into a bloody mask, and as I passed, the lance shot past my ear, and fell across my shoulders to bounce down my back and off the rump of my mount. A horse was struggling on the ground, directly in my path, a man trapped underneath it, so I did the only thing I could. Knowing that if I swerved I'd probably fall off, we went straight over the fallen animal and its rider in a leap that I could never have made again if I'd tried for twenty years.

Despite being terrified, I was still exhilarated and began to realize what it was that Sykes had seen in the cavalry. The swift forward movement of the bunched horses was as exciting as flying in an aeroplane in and out of the folds of the earth. I could hear yells and screams and the clash of weapons. One of the Cossack ponies went down with a scream and I saw the sergeant swing his sabre at a running man. It caught him alongside the neck in a scything sweep and he went down with his head almost severed from his body. Machikov was still close alongside me and on the other side of Munro the big sergeant was still hemming him in, making sure we weren't stopped.

As we burst clear, all I could see were riderless horses and running men in the mist. The Cossacks were riding them down, cutting at them with wild swings of their swords, but Machikov and the sergeant didn't change direction until we were clear of the mêlée, then they reined in, crowding their horses against ours so that we had to slow down, too.

'Och, ma God!' Munro said, his face haggard.

Machikov grinned. 'Is good, no?' he said.

The horses came to a stop with their hooves clattering across a stony road. The sergeant stayed with us while Machikov went back into the mist to round up his men. After a while, they reappeared, leading a string of riderless horses and driving before them a dozen Red cavalrymen they'd captured. It was just beginning to become daylight and, as a small breeze sprang up, the mist began to clear.

Machikov insisted on going back to the scene of the fight but I could see the roofs and domes of Tsaritsyn just to the south and would much have preferred to continue in that direction. The plain to the north seemed quite empty. Two or three men were running as fast as they could through the grass and flowers and Machikov nodded to the sergeant. I didn't look but I heard screams and when I raised my eyes there were no running men.

Munro's face was white. 'Ah dinnae like this sort o' war,' he said.

The Cossacks gathered their prisoners into a group and made them take off their boots and uniforms then, stripped to their underclothing, they drove them into a bunch.

'For God's sake,' Munro said and, for a minute, as I thought he was going to object, I grabbed his bridle and held on to it. I knew what was going to happen but I knew we could do nothing about it.

There was the clatter of rifle bolts and the Cossacks fired into the group of terrified, shivering men, and the whole lot seemed to recoil into themselves, finally sinking to their knees and rolling over. The Cossacks didn't seem to think there was anything odd in what they'd done and merely bent over the scattered clothing and boots, trying them on, laughing and shoving at each other, apparently oblivious to the dying men a few yards away.

As they climbed back into the saddle, two of the Bolsheviks struggled to their feet. Machikov turned and stared at them for a moment, then he drew a revolver and, even as they begged for mercy, he shot each through the head.

'*Kak zhal.* What a pity!' He turned and grinned at me. 'Only *Bolsheviki,*' he ended. 'Now we go. Good morning.'

I stared after him. I'd thought once before that this was a different kind of war. Now I was sure it was.

Chapter 5

It took us quite a while to get back to the squadron because the Cossacks took us to their camp and insisted on trying to get us drunk on vodka, and when we finally reached the train it was dark again. The warnings that had been passed out about Bolshevik saboteurs had been well heeded and the sentry's call came at once.

'Who goes there?'

'Santa Claus,' Munro shouted, 'eight reindeers an' ten other silly beggars.'

'Pass, friends,' the sentry said and he was grinning all over his face as we came into view.

'Nice to see you back, sir,' he told me. 'We all thought you'd gone.'

Everybody in the mess was in the deepest gloom, firmly convinced we'd been killed or at least captured by the Red cavalry. They'd all seen Munro land and me go down after him but, because of the mist, they'd been unable to send out a DH9 and when we hadn't reappeared they'd feared the worst.

Slingsby was eating when we arrived and he leapt up immediately and started yelling. Everyone appeared at once, asking questions and shouting, and Slingsby started to torment Munro as he usually did.

'Come on, you jolly old braw bricht moonlicht nit,' he said. 'You've just come back from the field of battle, so tell us about it. Recount your startling adventures. Have you lost any limbs? Is your head still firmly fixed in place? How did you escape? Use wet hen tactics? Go for them flat out with your head down so they didn't know what to do? It's always good for the blood pressure – yours, even if not theirs.'

Munro put on his wise old warrior act. 'Aye, ye do have tae use y'r head a bit,' he agreed.

'What makes you think you think with your head?' Slingsby yelled. 'If you get a bullet in the backside, I bet you'd find it a pretty disturbing thought, in spite of its situation. You should be careful. *The paths of glory lead but to the grave. So little Eric shouldn't try to be too brave.*'

Within a couple of days the shock of the killings we'd seen had washed over me. I'd seen death in greater quantity in France, and, despite the cruelty, I'd long since accepted that this was no ordinary war we were fighting in. For sheer hatred it had France beaten into a cocked hat and the Cossacks could never be judged by the standards by which we'd judged European soldiers.

Munro seemed less happy. He'd had another letter from Barbara Hatherley asking when he was coming home. She'd finally persuaded her parents that he'd make a good husband, it seemed, and was actually in the process of gathering things for her wedding, in what was known as 'her bottom drawer'. Munro showed me her letter. 'Mother's decided that we can have their piano,' she ended.

'Well, that's something,' I said. 'You'll be able to entertain her with all those awful songs you used to entertain us with. Played as badly as only you know how.'

There was also a letter for me and I knew at once that it was from Charley because it was written in that bold hand of hers with a pen nib that seemed as wide as a shovel. It seemed to go with Charley – bold, forthright and courageous – and I turned it over to look at the flap of the envelope. As usual it had SWASK written on it. She'd often had to write letters home for soldiers in the hospitals in France and had got used to putting SWALK – Sealed With A Loving Kiss – on the back for them. This was her own personal sign: 'Sealed,' she always said, 'with a smacking kiss.'

The letter came from the South of France and contained the news that her family was heading home again, despite the fact that the season had only just started.

'Prices are too high,' she reported, 'and a slump's starting at home. The parents are talking of getting a cottage in the country. We never had *much* money, but now we've got less so I'm going back to nursing. Judging by the way things are going, by the time you come back, I'll probably be a matron. I miss you, if only because there's no one around to have a real ding-dong battle with. A man asked me to marry him last week. His name was Ronnie Witherspoon, which probably explains why I said, "Not likely".'

There was a lot more in the same vein, all breezy, cheerful and optimistic as she always was, and I was so homesick in the empty spaces of the steppes I felt as bad as Munro.

We scraped up all the whisky we could spare and went into Tsaritsyn to hand it over to the Cossacks who'd rescued us. Deciding it wouldn't be a good idea to be around when they started drinking it, it was my plan to hand it over and bolt.

As we approached the town, we passed a large house with all its windows broken and hammers and sickles daubed on the whitewash.

'Yon's no' paint,' Munro said bleakly. 'Paint doesnae attract flies.'

The inside stank of stale spirits and the marble walls were chipped, while the heads of a whole row of stone nymphs on either side of a broad staircase had been carefully broken off. Heavily nailed boots had ruined the shepherdesses on a tapestry that had been used for a rug and the parquet floor of the hall was covered with horse manure as though the Red cavalry had used it as a stable.

Priceless books had been burned to provide warmth and one of the 47 Squadron men, who was also prowling around, said there was a grave in the grounds with fourteen bodies in it.

Tsaritsyn was a ghost town. Human bodies, horses, even pet dogs, lay in every street, and you could smell the odour of decay everywhere so that it was as bad as No Man's Land in France. The shops were empty and every church was smashed or burned, while the people were drifting hopelessly about, as though bewildered to find themselves alive. Outside the town was a huge ditch which was said to contain thousands of victims of Red butchery, some of them buried so shallowly their hands and feet were sticking through the surface.

'Let's get out of here,' Munro said in a taut edgy voice.

We didn't deliver the whisky after all but sent a message to Machikov telling him we'd lay on a party for them with 47 Squadron, at which they could drink all the whisky they could manage. We'd found a big house that hadn't been badly damaged and were using it as a communal mess, and when the Cossacks turned up we made a pretty odd mixture, with the RAF men in their drab uniforms and smooth English faces and the Cossacks with their beards, moustachios and fierce eyes.

We did it in style, however, and Sykes had even come up from Ekaterinodar for the occasion.

Caviare and other Russian dishes had been set out on tables among the glasses and there was even some champagne, though the Cossacks scorned this and went straight for the whisky. There was plenty to eat and Shkura's men tucked into it as though they were starving, shifting the cutlets and *borscht* and wheatflour pancakes as if they hadn't eaten for years. After a while it began to grow noisy and I got Sykes on one side as an excuse to dodge the drinking. He was worried.

Wrangel wanted to consolidate and strengthen the White reserves before advancing. Denikin, however, wanted to go full steam ahead for Moscow while Wrangel headed for Saratov, Sidorin's Army of the Don headed for Voronezh, and Mai-Maievski's Volunteer Army headed further west via Kursk, Orel and Tula.

'Wrangel thinks he's taking too big a chance,' Sykes said. 'He's dividing his command and not one of his armies is strong enough to hold off the Reds if they're attacked separately. Wrangel's won a tremendous victory here and it would be much more sensible to hang on to it and build up. Any other way, we've got no organized base and

Wrangel's not strong enough to take Saratov on his own.'

By this time, people were making speeches, most of them not waiting for the last one to finish. Toasts began and the Russians drank them as if the end of the world were due within an hour. The orchestra we'd hired began to play a haunting melody that was easy to pick up and the Cossacks began to sing in deep basses and baritones.

'Is the song of "Stenka",' Pudhovkhin said. 'Is much good song. Very Russian. Very sad. All people sing it.'

Everyone in the room was shouting the refrain, even the RAF men trying to join in, then Munro, with a wild look in his eye, pushed the pianist aside and began to pound out the old songs he'd played in Flying Corps messes all the way across France. The Russians attempted to sing the choruses but they were foxed until he started on 'Ochen Tchornye', which everybody knew – even the British who called it 'Black Eyes'. Then he played 'Tipperary' and they knew that, too, and finally he went into 'If You Were The Only Girl In The World', 'Long Long Trail' and 'Keep The Home Fires Burning', which had just the right amount of melody and sadness to please the Russians. Heaven knows what he finished off with but eventually everybody was roaring out the words.

The party was growing wilder and bowls of caviare were upset and plates smashed. Shkura's men were drinking straight from the bottle now and some of them were even beginning to weep.

'We Russians are much sentimental,' Pudhovkhin explained.

After a while dancing started. The dancers were Machikov's bearded ruffians in their long-skirted *tcherkasses* with the cartridge cases across their chests and draped with inlaid swords and daggers. The accordions, violins and balalaikas played faster and faster and they began to perform extraordinary feats with the razor-sharp *khinzhals*, which they managed somehow to clash together while holding them in their teeth. There seemed to be daggers tucked into collars and sleeves, between each two fingers – behind ears, it seemed, even up nostrils.

They began to do a sort of knees-bend dance, shooting out their feet in front of them, yelping all the time while the room shook to the pounding of tables. The music grew wilder and wilder and everyone began to clap and shout. One of the

Russians slid out of sight and a table collapsed, but the dancers just went on, and I doubt if a salvo of heavy artillery would have stopped them. Then, as the music reached a crescendo and ended in a terrific crash, the dancers rose in a tremendous leap and while still in the air, divested themselves of all their daggers which flew in every direction.

Determined not to be outdone, Slingsby, who had had the Cossacks' mouths open as he produced bullets or bowls of caviare from out of their beards or under their arms, stood up, his pale eyes wild, his colourless hair on end, his cherub face pink with devilment, and borrowed a couple of Cossack sabres which he crossed on the floor.

'What in Heaven's name's he going to do?' Sykes asked.

'Och, ma God,' Munro said uneasily. 'Ah think it's a sword dance.'

'He'll cut his feet off! Those damn' things are like razors.'

But he didn't. Slingsby had more hidden talents than anyone knew about and his sword dance had the Cossacks howling with delight and even Munro pounding the table for more.

'Can't be done,' Slingsby panted as he staggered from the floor. 'Too puffed! Exhausted and all that! Need to recuperate!'

Munro beamed at him. He had suddenly found a friend. 'Och, the fine wee boy!' he crowed. 'Ah reckon ye could do a Strip-the-willow in eighty-nine seconds flat and an eightsome reel in twenty-two, an' yon are records. Where did ye learn tae dance like that?'

'Stationed in Scotland for six months,' Slingsby gasped. 'Had a girl friend called MacNab.'

'You've made the evening,' Sykes laughed. 'They'll never think we're effete and decadent and unmanly again. What can I offer you? My castle? My lands? You could have my daughter's hand in marriage, but I haven't got one.'

'Oh—' Slingsby was recovering his breath now and was beginning to eye the food again '—just put me down for a VC if there's one going spare, sir. That'll do for now, except that you could pass that plate of *borscht*.'

The party was beginning to be dangerous now because Russian revolvers were being discharged at the ceiling. And with every toast – and there seemed to be dozens of them: to the King, to the dead Tsar, to Wrangel, to the British Mission, to the White Army, to the gallant RAF, to your mother, your next-door neighbour, your best girl, anything anyone could think of – the glasses hurtled in a shower against the walls.

'*Na Moskvu! Na Moskvu!* To Moscow! To Moscow by Christmas!' The yelling was becoming hysterical and Sykes looked at me sadly.

'I just hope they get there,' he said.

—

None of us felt at his best the following morning, but fortunately there was no flying because Wrangel was busily scraping up troops for the attack he'd been ordered to make on Saratov, and he came to visit us to express his thanks for what we'd done. He was a long lean greyhound of a man, with a tremendous personality and like many of the Russian nobility was of German descent. When the revolution had started he'd been imprisoned in Petrograd and mutinous sailors and Red Guards had wanted to shoot him because, while other officers had worn red ribbons to save their lives, he'd refused. Despite his enormous height and commanding presence, he'd borne a charmed life and when he was finally arrested, his wife had refused to leave his side so that, while over a thousand officers were murdered, somehow Wrangel was freed, escaping with his family and even the family jewels which he'd hidden in the stomachs and heads of his daughter's dolls.

He made no bones about his dislike for Denikin's strategy. 'He's an infantry officer,' he said, 'and he's trying to fight an infantry war. This is a cavalry war. And we have too many people behind us who are tradesmen and profiteers and not soldiers.'

Even we knew he was right because the Whites had enough men to beat the Reds easily if only some of the enormous numbers of splendidly dressed officers in soft jobs had been prepared to serve in the ranks for a while.

'Perhaps it's as well they don't, though,' Sykes said. 'Most of them are nothing but scented popinjays.'

'Aye,' Munro growled. 'Fillin' their pockets sellin' army supplies. We've all seen regimental trains like circus convoys wi' the loot and the hangers-on they carry.'

With some units existing only on paper, brigades as big as battalions, and batteries with enough horses for only two guns, it was depressing to think that all the fighting of the spring might be wasted.

Fortunately, Charley's letters were coming now in a steady stream. She was back in England and working at Guy's, which was quite a change for a girl who before the war had had no thought in her head except for clothes, dancing and riding to hounds.

'The British aristocracy's always been quick to shove its finger into every pie worth having,' Sykes smiled. 'We're always quicker than most to adopt new methods. That's probably why we haven't had a revolution in England.'

Munro had also received a bundle of letters but they only seemed to depress him further. 'Brat,' he said. 'Ah'm worried. What would ye think o' me if Ah applied tae go home?'

'I'd think you'd got more sense than I ever realized,' I said. 'If this new attack goes wrong, we're going to have quite a job getting out of Russia.'

'But it's no' so easy as that, is it? Would it no' seem as if Ah were dodgin' the difficult bits? Suppose the fellers think Ah'm afraid?'

I tapped the ribbons on his chest. Two of them were for gallantry. 'You don't get a chest like that for being afraid, old son,' I pointed out. 'Perhaps you need a rest.'

'Aye, there's no' a smile in me. Perhaps Ah'm no' the blood-and-guts merchant Ah thought Ah was, because sometimes Ah rather fancy havin' a nice nine-to-fiver again and gaein' home tae a warm fire and a wee dram. Mebbe Ah'm growin' old.'

I made up my mind. 'I'll tell Sykes I'm invaliding you home,' I said. 'For heaven's sake, man, it requires half the squadron strength to hoist you into the cockpit, pick up your sticks, and get you to your feet when you fall over.'

He seemed to recover his spirits with his reprieve. He was a lot older than the rest of us and it was my opinion that he'd had enough. RAF doctors were years ahead of the Army and Navy in the study of combat fatigue and they'd decided long since that courage was like the sand in an hour-glass. After a time it leaked away and I decided Munro had reached that point and was better where he was safe.

That night he appeared outside the train with an upright piano he'd found in a wrecked house. It was badly scarred but apart from one or two notes in the bottom octaves that didn't seem to work, it functioned quite well.

'What are you gonna do with that?' Tucker asked him.

Munro shook his head. 'Ah've missed ma music,' he pointed out.

'You never knew the first thing about music,' Slingsby said.

'Ah did so!' He looked indignant. 'Was I no' a piper in the Territorials before I joined this misbegotten outfit? Mon, wi' "Johnny Cope" Ah could hae the whole battalion wide awake at dawn and standin' on their feet in two seconds flat.'

'Heads pounding,' Slingsby said. 'Nerves shattered, fingers in ears, and hair on end like an electric shock at the sheer appalling din. Did no one ever tell you, Jock, that bagpipes sound like strangled moggies?'

Munro glared. 'Ah'll have ye know,' he said, 'that Ah've had men weepin'. Ah lairned ma pipin' from a feller who'd been a pipe-major in the Gordons and ye should hae haird him on "Flowers of the Forest". Mon, it fair made y'r hair curl wi' the sorrow of it.'

There was a bullet hole through the piano's front panel and someone had wrenched off the brass candle-holders, but we hoisted it into the saloon and, after a preliminary canter up and down the keyboard, Munro was happily pounding away on it.

> *"And when Ah tell them*
> *How wonderful y'are,*
> *They'll never believe me—"*

He'd never been a pianist, but he had a marvellous ability to rouse people from their gloom and he soon had the whole flight roaring away. We were just in the middle of what looked like developing into a splendid party when Pudhovkhin appeared with half a dozen nurses from Train Number 643 which had appeared down the line a mile away to carry the Tsaritsyn wounded south. Olga was among them but, as Tucker headed for her, somehow she managed to slip past him and landed up on one of the banquettes alongside me.

She looked tired and thin and her eyes seemed bigger than ever. 'We are going back to Ekaterinodar,' she said.

'I think is best,' Pudhovkhin agreed. 'If something goes wrong here, this no place to be.'

He passed us a drink and discreetly disappeared.

'I am glad we have meet again,' Olga said shyly.

'Me too.'

'You have girl in England?'

'Yes.' We started to swop photographs. 'Have you got a boy?'

She shook her head. 'He is murdered in Petrograd in 1917.'

I didn't know what to say. You were always coming up against these appalling tragedies of the revolution, and they always left you speechless because there never was anything to say in reply.

'He has a good family,' she went on. 'They were kind, and when the revolution comes, the servants try to smuggle them to safety. It is not their own people who murder them. It is sailors from the docks.'

I was glad when Munro started playing the piano again. He started off with 'Ochen Tchornye', which wasn't really a good choice for a party because it had a sad note about lost loves, then he went into 'Stenka Razin', which he'd managed to pick up, and that wasn't the jolliest of tunes either. But then he realized that no one was smiling and plunged into the old popular tunes and Strauss waltzes, and everyone knew those. Tucker grabbed Olga and started dancing with her and Slingsby grabbed one of the other nurses and in no time they were all jigging around. There wasn't much room but we managed very well.

I found myself dancing with Olga again – not once but several times – and I saw Tucker in a corner, his eyes faintly reproachful like a dog that wasn't allowed to come in out of the rain. Then I noticed that Olga was holding me a little tighter as we danced, and had her cheek against mine and I grew a little worried because I was thinking of Charley and had no desire to get involved.

I walked back with her to the hospital train and standing in the darkness I realized she was waiting for me to kiss her. I managed a half-hearted peck on her cheek and she started crying softly, before turning and running up the steps.

Pudhovkhin was waiting alone in the saloon when I got back. He looked serious.

'You are perhaps in love with my sister, Sir Major?' he asked.

I shook my head. 'No, Puddy,' I said. 'I'm sorry but I'm not.'

'I think she becomes in love with you.'

I nodded. 'I think so, too. I didn't want it that way.'

He smiled, the melancholy deepening in his eyes. 'We Russians are much sentimental and romantic.'

'I think you're right. But I have a girl in England, and what would happen when I went home? She'd be much wiser to fall for one of her own nationality.'

He sighed and drew a deep breath. 'I would like her to marry an Englishman, you know, Sir Major.'

It startled me. 'Oh? Why?'

'Because then she would have British nationality. And that, I think, would be safer if things go wrong.'

'I'm sorry, Puddy.'

He drew a deep breath. 'You see, Sir Major, as a little girl, always she dreamed of fairies and living happily ever after. I think what has happened has seemed so impossible to her. Always she was protected and I would like her to have some of this sort of life in the future because, you see, I don't think I shall survive this campaign.'

'You might if you flew a Camel,' I said.

'No.' He shook his head. 'Is nothing to do with that. It is fate. All Russians know about this. I have seen it clearly. Alexei Ivanovitch Pudhovkhin will not survive.'

He made one last try. 'It would not be for long.'

I looked at him quickly. 'What wouldn't be for long?'

He shrugged. 'Other girls make the arrangements with British soldiers. They agree to leave them and end the marriage the minute they are out of Russia. It is—' he shrugged '—just an arrangement, that's all.'

I'd heard of such arrangements but I could just imagine what Charley would say if I arrived on her doorstep with a Russian girl on my arm. She was broad-minded but I didn't think she was as broad-minded as all that.

'Perhaps one of the others,' I said. 'Perhaps Tucker.'

He shrugged and gave me a sad smile. 'I think she has romantic ideas about *you*, Sir Major.' He sighed. 'It is a pity, because I think Denikin will not get to Moscow and Wrangel, good as he is, will not take Saratov.'

–

Puddy was right. Wrangel didn't take Saratov and his troops were forced back to Kamyshin. Reinforcing his men, he tried again and his Cossacks did in the end manage to get into the place and take thirteen thousand prisoners, but it was a hollow victory with a lot of casualties and no certainty of remaining there.

It was late summer now with the burning lands of the Don shimmering in the heat haze. Girls were harvesting the sunflower seeds and trying to sell us enormous green melons whose pink flesh held the germs of cholera. The burning wind had scorched the earth and the grass was shrivelled and yellow, while the road alongside the railway track was cracked and rutted with concrete-like dried mud. The flowers had disappeared with the heat and the whole steppe was empty of everything but tawny grass and clumps of birch and alder.

The hot weather had started up the typhus again. It had always been dormant in the White armies and the heat had set it going once more so that the hospitals were full of patients, lying on straw in bare rooms, the reddish brown rash of the disease across their entire bodies. Some of them were raving, and sick and wounded lay side by side, gasping for breath and feebly fighting off the flies. None of them seemed to have been washed since their arrival and they were still in infected uniforms caked with dust and sweat, because bandages and lint simply didn't exist in the White forces and their place was taken by wads of straw, cotton rags and strips torn from clothing.

Both squadrons were busy, strafing the rear areas and bombing the Red columns and railways to the north. Munro seemed to have recovered from his depression with the knowledge that he'd eventually be going home, and even seemed to enjoy flying again. I was careful to see that he wasn't sent on the more dangerous jobs and in Slingsby, despite the mad look in his eye, I found a very useful lieutenant who took his place naturally and easily. We had no casualties and only a few holes in our machines.

Wrangel was desperately wanting to pull back while he still could but he was ordered to continue with his advance despite the fact that he was receiving no reinforcements and had far too few men. Then in late July, the Red Army counter-attacked and though, after three days' fighting, Budenny's cavalry was thrown back, it was obvious to everyone that the victory had cost Wrangel too many men and that, with a few more such 'victories', he'd be forced on the defensive for lack of troops.

On 1 August, the Reds started attacking again all along the line and it was like the German advance in the spring of 1918 all over again, with the Camels in the air as long as it was daylight, attacking troop trains and Red reinforcements to allow Wrangel to fall back to Tsaritsyn. Though the Red Air Force wasn't very good, there was always the usual mixed bag of machines, often with the brown Fokker DVII in the lead. The White Russian DH9 crews hadn't improved much and often got us into tricky situations by their carelessness and indifference, and on one rotten day we lost two of them and Slingsby, because we had to go in low and rescue them from under a couple of flights of Albatroses and Spads.

Slingsby managed to make his way back in style, sitting on a farm cart driven by a remarkably pretty peasant girl, with his machine hitched by its tail to the back, but the DH9 crews were all killed, one of them a man called Dmitriov who was the best balalaika player in a country full of good balalaika players.

We all went to the funerals in Tsaritsyn, a community affair with the white-painted coffins – placed on white-painted carts pulled by white-shrouded, white-plumed horses – led by priests flanked by a chorus of psalm singers and acolytes carrying pictures of the saints.

The following day we ran into the same bunch of Reds again.

–

The hospital train was due to leave that night for the south and, during the evening, Puddy had brought his sister over for tea with another nurse. It was while they were there that we got an alarm message to the effect that the Russian DH9s were in trouble again, and we left them flat, running out to the aeroplanes, looking tremendously dramatic as we charged away to do battle and taking off in a cloud of dust.

We soon saw the Red machines, this time with a Fokker triplane and a Pfalz we'd not seen before, and our old friend, the brown Fokker, in the lead. The DH9s were five miles away bolting for home with the Red planes dropping out of the sky like a set of vultures behind them. I fired a Very light and swung towards them.

Time was short and we went in without waiting to ask questions. I saw two Red Nieuports flutter down and began to wonder if perhaps the Russians weren't finding it a little disheartening fighting against crack RAF squadrons blooded in France, but the odds were against us a little this time and I saw Munro go limping away to safety. I sat above the fight till he was safely to the south and, as I went down to join in again, Slingsby, who was developing into quite a flyer, seemed to be flying three ways at once, taking pot shots at a Spad, a triplane and the Pfalz. As he broke clear, the Pfalz's rudder came off and it went down out of control, then the pilot of the brown Fokker, who'd been doing what I'd been doing and sitting on the fringe of the fight waiting for a victim, pounced.

Slingsby was in trouble at once and I went down after the Fokker in a dive that made the Camel shudder. As Slingsby broke away to safety, the Fokker swung out and the next moment we were going round in a ding-dong ring-a-roses firing snapshots at each other whenever the opportunity offered.

It was late now and the sky seemed to be filled with towering mountains of purple and blood-red. The Fokker was above me, swinging in a swift shadow against the dark-pillared gateway of a crimson castle, black-purple against the light, its wings and spars outlined with fire. Glancing up, I saw its nose drop as it tried to get into position behind me and snatched the Camel round to the left. Turning to the right, the Camel could swivel on a sixpence because of the torque of the big engine, so I allowed the Fokker to close up then pulled the Camel viciously the other way. The earth, misty blue beneath me, swung like a plate, and the Fokker shot beneath me in a flash of vermilion, the fabric rippling along the fuselage. In a second we were facing each other.

I'd suspected for a long time that the Fokker pilot was a German, because he handled his machine well, and I saw flickers of light behind the propeller and a bullet clanked on the Camel's radiator. Above the high crackle of the Camel's engine, I caught the howl of the Fokker's BMW as it swept past and saw the bright red splash of the star on its wings. There was a faint brief glimpse of oil streaks alongside the engine then the Camel, with its remarkable agility, was round and behind and just above, so close I felt I could have thrown a spanner into the Fokker's cockpit. The pilot's head swung round and his goggles became two large red eyes as the sun caught the glass and the bony angles of his face.

He was trying hard to escape now, swimming sideways, it seemed, as aeroplanes always appear to when their courses aren't the same, bathed in a red glow that came through the clouds. As he went round, I went round after him, the Camel shuddering with its speed; and frustrated by all the turning, he tried to go the other way. As he slid in front of me I pressed the triggers and saw an aileron tear loose, then, as the pilot heaved desperately at the joystick I felt a jar and knew we'd collided and my wheels had touched him.

Swinging away, I looked to see what damage had been done, but everything seemed to be normal around me and I peered over the side of the cockpit for the Fokker. For a moment it seemed to have disappeared, then I saw it far below me, still bathed in that blood-red glow from the setting sun. As I watched, the top wing crumpled where it had caught my undercarriage and it began to go down in a gentle curve, shedding fragments of wood and fabric as it went. Then the surface of the wing began to peel off like a skin and the whole structure collapsed. The Fokker's nose dropped at once and it disappeared towards the earth, with just one large crumpled wing going down after it, sliding from side to side like a falling leaf in autumn, picking up the red glow from the sun every time it tilted towards the west.

I had lost the wreckage in the shadows of the earth but then I caught a spot of red as it hit the ground and flared into flame, and as I looked round I realized everybody else had vanished and I was alone in a waning crimson glow as the clouds closed over the sun.

I picked up the railway track and after about a quarter of an hour's flying saw the lights of the squadron train, and turned to make my landing.

I came in low out of a darkening sky and as the Camel settled and the wheels touched, the one the Fokker had hit collapsed. The nose went down and the propeller flew to pieces as the tip caught the ground. Dust and earth flew up and the machine began to slew wildly, wires twanging, struts groaning and squeaking, a spray of grass flying into the air. Finally it stood on its nose, rocked back on to its tail and came to a stop.

Slingsby was alongside me in a moment, a shadowy figure throwing off the harness straps, and I heard Munro yelling in the background as they dragged me out. I'd banged my eyebrow and split it open so that there was blood on my face and I felt dizzy, but Tucker plucked me free with his huge fists and not very gently slammed me to the ground. As the lights stopped flashing, I was aware of perfume and found myself looking up dazedly into Olga's huge eyes. They were full of tears and she was dabbing away at the blood.

'Oi, Marteen,' she was saying. 'Marteen, Marteen!'

Over her shoulder I could see Tucker watching her, and there was a blank, tragic expression on his face. Then Munro realized what he was thinking and had the brains to make a joke of it to break the silence. He gave Tucker a shove and gave a yell of laughter.

'Och,' he yelled, 'yon feller's only got tae waggle his eyebrows at 'em and they fall for him in heaps. It's a guid job it never lasts.'

Chapter 6

For some time Tucker seemed to avoid me in the mess and I wasn't sorry because I wasn't sure what I ought to say to him. What had happened was none of my doing but he seemed to be thinking that it was, and he was vaguely resentful because he and Puddy had become close friends and he seemed to suspect some sort of treachery.

'It is unrequited love,' Puddy said cheerfully. 'Do you think is Russian blood in him?'

'Wi' a name like Tucker?' Munro said. 'Och, awa wi' ye!'

Puddy glanced at Tucker who was sitting on the platform at the end of the mess car, mooning at the horizon as if he were sick.

'Is very Russian, nevertheless,' he said, shaking his head. 'We are great believers in tragedy and fate. Is in all our songs and poems. We give ourselves wholeheartedly to pleasure and happiness – and death.'

I felt like telling him to go and boil his head. What was wrong with Tommy wasn't fate or Russia. It was plain unadulterated calf-love, and I knew how he was feeling because it was something I'd suffered from myself on and off until I'd met Charley. Tommy had just got it bad, and it worried me because we had no room for a lovesick pilot whose mind might well be on other things when he needed his wits about him. So far we'd escaped casualties and I was hoping to keep it that way.

'*Na Moskvu*' seemed to have gone out of fashion suddenly. Disturbing rumours kept making their way back from the front and every time we flew we could see with our own eyes the White troops streaming southwards. We all knew that Wrangel was setting up his headquarters in Tsaritsyn again, and, still not getting the reinforcements he needed, had even ordered the evacuation of the city.

With his *muzhik* blouse and high-peaked cap, he was everywhere at once. Strict orders had gone out that nothing but arms and ammunition were to leave, followed only by the civil and military administrations, and last of all by those civilians who wished to go, but the wealthy still managed to fill trains with household goods, paintings, furs, furniture, even cars and pianos. Whenever he found out Wrangel came down on them like an avenging angel, tossing all the private property on to the track and emptying locked trucks whose documents, issued by bribed officials, claimed they were filled with munitions.

By 18 August, the town was empty of military units, stores and ammunition, and our machines, like 47 Squadron's, had been loaded on the flat cars ready to start south. A group of Kalmuk cavalrymen went by on their shaggy ponies, their narrow black eyes expressionless, their yellow faces fixed. They were moving slowly, led by an officer who was wearing a greatcoat. Then, behind them, a cart full of wounded appeared and the driver seemed to be panicking because it passed us at full speed, heading for the hospital trains further along the track. The wounded men's heads were jolting as the wheels struck the ruts in the bone-hard ground and they were screaming for mercy as the bumps jarred their wounds. The driver took no notice, however, and the Kalmuks had to scatter from his path, their harnesses jingling, their swords slapping against their saddles.

Something in the driver's manner worried us and we watched the cart disappear with anxious eyes. It only needed a few more like him, I thought, and the whole army would take off.

We were still awaiting the signal to leave when I saw a car approaching through a cloud of dust, the front wheels wobbling from side to side as they struck the ruts that had shaken the load of wounded. It was Sykes, and Collishaw was with him. They'd come up by train from Ekat and, while they'd been conferring, a message had arrived from Wrangel to hold us. Reinforcements had come unexpectedly and, with Kuban regiments still in control a few miles to the north, Wrangel had changed his mind.

We unloaded the Camels at full speed and went back into action, and though we flew endlessly, we were still called out again as soon as we'd landed and had snatched a meal and something to drink. The Reds were growing cleverer now, though, and when we strafed them, instead of standing there and letting us, they scattered or hid in the folds of the ground, while batteries of machine-guns were always mounted and ready to fire back. In addition, the Red Air Force seemed to be growing a little more daring and 47 Squadron's landing strip was strafed by Red fighters while they were in the air to the north, and six men were killed. But the big Red attack set up by Budenny had faded out with enormous losses of men and material and, rather to our surprise, everybody began to toast '*Na Moskvu*' once more because Denikin had pushed so far north his lines stretched from Poltava through Kharkov to Kamyshin, and he was only three hundred and seventy-five miles from Moscow which, in terms of Russian distances, was on the doorstep. Into the bargain, Yudenich was attacking in the north-west; and in Siberia, after an initial setback, Kolchak was rallying. It began to look once more as though the campaign might really end in victory.

'Now perhaps ye'll cheer up, Puddy,' Munro said slapping Pudhovkhin on the back. 'We're winnin', mon.'

Puddy shrugged. 'Perhaps,' he said. 'But *I* shall not reach Moscow.'

Somehow he seemed like a pagan African who'd been told by a witch doctor that a voodoo had been laid on him and that he was going to die.

Three days later, he disappeared.

We flew north towards Saratov and just south of the city met the usual mixed bag of machines. There was a wild mêlée and the last I saw of Puddy he was mixing it with another Albatros and seemed to be getting easily the best of it. But when, as always happened, the sky suddenly emptied and I started looking round for the rest of the flight, he'd disappeared.

The others formed up on me one after the other, first Slingsby, then Tucker, an enormous figure bulging out of his machine, followed by Munro and the others. But the black Albatros was missing and when we landed one of the Russian DH9 observers said he'd seen it land safely miles from nowhere.

'For God's sake, where?' I demanded.

But, of course, typically, he'd not thought either to signal us or to make a note of the spot and could only point towards the north.

'I want two DH9s,' I said. 'One with a full crew. I'll fly the other.'

Major Rhatanyi appeared, smelling strongly of scent and looking as though he'd just stepped out of a gentleman's outfitters with his leg-of-mutton breeches and wasp-waisted tunic. He was dead against lending me his machines.

'Why?' I snapped.

'Because you cannot fly a De Havilland.'

'F'r God's sake, mon,' Munro snapped, 'if it's got wings, Brat can fly it!'

Rhatanyi was still unwilling, and I finally had to threaten to blow his head off with my revolver before he agreed. The observer who'd seen Puddy go down climbed into the rear cockpit of the machine I was to fly and the other took off with its rear cockpit containing ballast and spares hastily thrown in by Flight-Sergeant Merry. Taxiing into the wind I pushed the throttle open and as the engine roared, the machine moved forward, the long wings dipping and swaying, their tips quivering as it rolled over the uneven ground. As it gathered speed, I moved the stick forward to lift the tail, then pulled back on it and the rumbling stopped as the wheels left the ground.

Below, as far as I could see, was the level plain of the steppe with Tsaritsyn over on my right. The light was brilliant and I knew there should be no problem in finding Puddy, because his machine would stand out in all that emptiness like a candle on a Christmas cake. But, as I yelled back and forth in a frustrated argument with the Russian observer, I realised that he had really no idea where to look. Then Tommy Tucker, ranging out towards the west, came back, waggled his wings and pointed, and immediately, I swung the DH9 after him, followed by the other two-seater and the rest of the flight.

The black Albatros was there all right but it had been burned and lay broken-backed and scorched, in the immense empty melancholy of the steppe. In the unrelieved flatness you could see it for miles and I knew that if I could see it so could the Bolsheviks.

Circling it warily, watching the distance for cavalry patrols, I signed to Munro that I was going down and that the Camels were to provide cover. Munro waved back and I landed alongside the wreckage, swung the machine round and taxied back to it, finally turning into wind ready for an immediate take-off. The other two-seater had landed just behind me and was now taxiing up alongside, waiting with its empty cockpit for Puddy to come running through the grass and climb aboard.

But there was no sign of Puddy so, wondering if it were a trap, I told the Russian observer to climb out and look around. He was a small man, his face half hidden by the heavy crash helmet he wore and he was clearly nervous.

'Get out!' I yelled.

He didn't want to and preferred to stand with his finger on the trigger of his guns, and I nearly had to drag him out of the cockpit by the scruff of the neck. There was no blood on the ground, as there would have been if Puddy had been hit, and I could only imagine that he'd tried to walk back to safety. There was no point in risking two machines and three lives by staying where I was so I signed to the observer to get back aboard.

We flew back in the same extended formation. I was cold with dread and livid with fury with that damned BHP engine which persisted in trying to cut out on me all the way back.

With Wrangel clinging on to Tsaritsyn, Olga's train was operating just to the north of the city, so I borrowed a car and drove out with Tommy and Munro to where it was standing. It was half-full of wounded and there was an ambulance and several carts alongside which had obviously just brought more men from the north. Dr Abramov, who was checking them in, met me on the steps, smiling, but when I told him why I was there, his smile died. 'You had better come into the lounge,' he said. 'I'll send for her.'

Olga entered the lounge smiling, and I knew at once he'd told her nothing and she thought I'd come simply to see her. She shook hands formally and suggested I should have a glass of tea.

I shook my head. 'Sit down, Olga. I've something to say to you.'

She sat down, still smiling, and my mind squirmed as I tried to decide how I was going to put it. When my brother had been killed in 1915, I'd had the job of telling the girl who was to have married him what had happened. It had been an ordeal then and this time was going to be worse because although Olga spoke English well it was not well enough to absorb tragedy and I had only a few words of Russian.

'It's Puddy,' I said, and she guessed at once why I was there. Her eyes went dead and empty.

'Sasha is dead!'

'He crashed,' I said. 'He was seen.'

She didn't say anything for a moment then she lifted her hands to her mouth and pressed them tightly over her lips as though to stop herself crying out, staring at me with those enormous eyes of hers. Then suddenly they welled over with tears and her face crumpled and she swayed so that I thought she was going to fall. I put my arms around her and she put her head on my shoulder and wept as if the sobs were tearing her apart.

'He is so good,' she managed. 'Always he is so good.'

I knew I mustn't stay because too much was beginning to happen too fast, and it seemed a good opportunity to throw Tommy Tucker in at the deep end. With his warm American's heart and his willingness to help and that surprising affection he continued to feel for Olga without any encouragement from her, he seemed the best person in the world just then to take care of her.

We left him sitting with his arm round her, offering her his handkerchief, his enormous bulk dwarfing her tiny frame. As we climbed into the car, Munro was in a gloomy mood.

'What yon swine do to their prisoners doesnae bear thinkin' aboot,' he said.

Sykes arrived two days later with a smooth-looking senior officer from the staff in Ekat to tell us what was happening.

'He'd be a damn sight more useful helping us to refuel the machines,' I growled. 'It's late August now. Winter starts early here so there's precious little flying weather left.'

The talk was less about the military situation than about Cossack hopes of setting up their own states. 'We have to accept,' the man from the Mission said, 'that the Cossacks aren't fighting for the return of the Tsar. They weren't very pleased when what they consider the decadent peoples of the north fled down to their territory from the revolution in Petrograd, and they're no more pleased now. Whether they're Don, Kuban or Terek Cossacks, they want independence and they don't think much of Denikin's slogan "Russia, One and Indivisible".'

He remained certain, however, despite the dissension, that we'd be in Moscow by Christmas. 'Everybody's moving forward now,' he said. 'Red Russia can't get much smaller without disappearing altogether.'

He'd brought a briefcase full of medals from Denikin and we held a parade at which, on behalf of the White Russian government, he gave me and Sykes the Tsarist Cross of St Vladimir and the white enamelled Cross of St George which, despite their fancy names, were good Russian decorations. Munro, Slingsby and Tucker and one or two of the DH9 pilots also received crosses and it appeared that 47 Squadron had also had their share.

'It's a lot o' medals for not much fighting,' I said and Munro grinned.

'They were a gey sight harder tae get in France,' he agreed.

'Of course,' the staff officer said in the mess afterwards, 'there's still a lot to be done and it's now becoming a three-dimensional war because a chap called Nestor Mahkno's started up an army called the Green Guards. They carry black flags and attack anybody and everybody – Reds, Whites, refugees, anything.' He reached for his coat because the day had been cheerless with a cold drizzle. 'They just add to the problems we have, because typhus seems to be spreading and I hear even Collishaw's got it.'

We were pleased to learn that the advance was to continue, but I remained uncertain and could only put my unformed worries down to the enormous size and emptiness of Russia which had that sort of effect on people. There seemed no immediate reason for fears, however, because with the future looking more secure, even Tsaritsyn was coming to life. Carriages were beginning to appear from nowhere, containing not only officers but women, too, dressed in fashionable clothes that they'd been hiding as they'd walked around under the Bolsheviks dressed to look as much like workers as they could. Even the mangy dogs had vanished and you could hear music again.

Munro began to look worried.

'What's bothering your baby mind, old fruit?' Slingsby asked.

'Och, Ah was just wonderin' if mebbe Ah should stick it oot wi' the rest of ye instead o' gaein' home.'

'Think nothing of it, darling. And don't, for Heaven's sake, let anyone suspect the taint of too much willingness. You know what they say: Never volunteer for anything. Juiceless cynics might call it enthusiasm.'

There was something in what Munro was feeling, all the same – a sense of unexpected security because the bodies that we'd seen when we'd first arrived had all gone and even the shops were starting to open. Then we heard that Denikin had taken Kursk only two hundred and eighty miles south of Moscow and the weight on our minds lifted a little more.

'I bet the Reds are shooting a few commissars for this lot,' Munro crowed. 'Perhaps even Trotsky himself. They havenae tae gae much further an' old Lenin'll be oot on his ear. Dictatorships never survive defeats.'

The cafes opened and it was even possible to see a good show because the place was full of refugee artistes from Moscow and Petrograd who had fled south with the revolution. Some of them had even sung or danced before the Tsar himself. The money remained impossible, of course, and you needed a barrowload just to pay for a meal. It had been printed like postage stamps so that you carried a couple of sheets with you and tore off what you wanted, and the notes were always spanking new as if they'd just come from the printers.

Some of the hotels were still partly wrecked, with boarded-up windows and shrapnel marks outside, and the furniture here and there was propped on boxes or books where a leg had been broken, but it was pleasant to see a little life again. At the back of my mind, however, I remained uneasy. Somehow, Denikin's advances seemed to have been too straightforward and Russia was far too big a place to stick your neck out too far. There were no trench lines as we'd known them in France – only strongposts and fortified towns and Budenny's cavalry were notoriously good at going round them.

Tucker never came with us into the town. With the improved news, Train Number 643 had remained in the area and he spent all his spare time with Olga. To see them walking together was amusing because his bulk made her seem twice as tiny, and she put her hand in his so trustingly I began to think that perhaps everything would be all right between them after all.

'Yon wee lad's got it bad,' Munro observed.

'For a canny Scot,' I said, 'it's taken you a long time to notice it.'

–

With little of the summer weather left for flying, flights were still regularly heading north and it was after one such flight of three machines that Munro arrived back in a state of wild excitement to bang his machine down cross-wind at a dangerous speed.

'It's him,' he yelled, scrambling from the cockpit.

'Who, for God's sake?' I said.

'Puddy! I saw him headin' this way on a pony.'

'Don't be damn' silly!'

His face went as red as a turkey-cock's. 'Ah'm no' bein' silly, ye great daft,' he yelled. 'Ah saw this feller on a pony just tae the north o' the city and he waved like mad! Ah went doon tae hae a look at him and Ah swear it was Puddy!'

It didn't seem possible, not after all this time, but it was worth taking a chance and I told Munro to refuel and sent him and his two men off again while I alerted the DH9 flight.

As we waited for Munro to return with confirmation, Tommy appeared from the hospital train. 'What's going on?' he demanded.

'Jock says he's seen Puddy.'

Tommy's face lit up. 'It can't be!' he said. 'But, gee, I sure hope it is!'

Munro was back within half an hour – alone – and he clambered awkwardly out of the cockpit to do his stiff-legged little dance. 'It *was* Puddy, mon,' he yelled. '*It – was – Puddy.*' His face grew sombre. 'But there was a wee bunch 'o' Red cavalry after him, Ah think. I left the others tae keep an eye on 'em while Ah came back tae report.'

Out of the corner of my eye I saw Tommy's Camel roar across the ground then sidle into the air in that peculiar crablike take-off of the Camel. As it disappeared to the north, I sent one of the flight mechs to round up the other pilots and told Flight-Sergeant Merry to refuel everybody and send them off again as soon as they arrived. Then I ran along the track to the British DH9 train because I wasn't going to trust the Russians again. Within a few minutes the whole lot of us were roaring off, me leading them in one of their machines with an empty rear cockpit.

Tommy was already out of sight and eventually we passed Munro's two Camels returning low on fuel. Soon afterwards we saw Tommy circling. As we approached, he pointed and waved, then jabbed a finger downwards, and we saw the solitary horseman trudging south. I went down for a closer scrutiny and it certainly looked like Puddy.

Then I spotted the Red cavalry in a dip only a mile or two to the north and wondered if they were using Puddy to get us within range. It seemed worth taking a chance.

I waved to the DH9s and as I dropped down to the solitary horseman I saw them circling to let go their bombs. I glanced upwards. The sky was clear and there appeared to be no enemy planes in sight. Tommy was still providing cover and Munro would be back within a short time.

I watched the ground change from a green-brown blur to individual blades of grass and felt the wheels rumble along the turf, then I swung the aircraft round in a big circle to see the horseman change direction and head for me. It *was* Puddy.

We didn't stop to exchange greetings and as he climbed aboard I immediately opened the throttle and swung the machine into the wind.

Then I saw the enemy fighters. They *had* been waiting and there seemed to be about a dozen of them, four of them breaking off to attack the De Havillands, while the rest kept coming straight for me. There was only Tommy above me at that moment and it looked very much as if we were going to have to rely on our own skill and the manoeuvrability of the DH.

'Gun, Puddy,' I screamed. 'Get the gun firing!'

Tommy was screaming down into the enemy fighters as hard as he could go and the whole flight split up. But there were too many of them and he couldn't handle them all, and the outside ones simply slipped past and kept on coming for us.

The rumble of the wheels stopped as I clawed the DH into the air, standing it on its wingtip in a climbing turn to swing it to the south. A Pfalz with a red star on its tail hurtled past and I heard Puddy fire a couple of short bursts then the gun stopped and as I glanced backwards, I saw he'd got a jam.

We were about five hundred feet up now and I decided it was safer to stay where I was instead of wasting time trying to climb any higher. The ground was racing back beneath us and I saw a line of trees shoot under the wingtip out of sight, then a man driving an ox-cart. He and his whole family looked up as we roared low over his head.

I felt a hand on my shoulder and heard Puddy screaming in my ear. '*Bolsheviki! Bolsheviki!*' I glanced round and saw the Pfalz coming down on my tail again. I waited until I gauged he was about to fire then stood the machine on its starboard wingtip and he shot past me, almost touching the ground with his wheels before he managed to pull up. But now I was facing a Spad and, as I swung away, I saw his tracers go through the wings. It wouldn't take much of this before we were in trouble. Then Tommy hurtled down between us so that the Spad had to turn away, and I swung south once more.

But the Pfalz was back again now and this time there was an Albatros alongside it. Away to the south I saw scattered dots in the sky and knew it was Munro on his way back with the others. Tommy was holding off the Spad but it would be several minutes before Munro could do anything to help and the situation was still nasty. As the two Red planes came down, I heard the gun behind me fire two or three short bursts then it stopped and, glancing round, I realized it had jammed again. I swung to the left and the Pfalz overshot once more but I was being carried into the path of the Albatros and, swinging back again, I almost hit the Pfalz which slipped in front of me, missing me by inches.

I'd been losing height all the time with all the manoeuvring and, with this small respite, I tried to climb again, but the Pfalz was back in no time with the Albatros still alongside. A quick glance round showed me that Tommy was fully occupied already and couldn't come to my assistance, but as the two machines swept in again, Munro and the others arrived. Immediately Slingsby broke out of formation and went for about nine at once, doing things with his machine I wouldn't have believed possible so that they scattered all over the sky.

The Pfalz was still there, though, and as he turned inwards, firing with all he'd got, I banked so that he missed and shot ahead of me yet again, then I saw tracers going though his wings and Munro's Camel howled over us so close I thought his wheels were going to tear the top wing off. The Pfalz swung away in desperation but we were all so low by this time that, as he lost height in his bank, he hit the ground with his wingtip. As it crumpled, the machine cartwheeled, end over end over end and a piece of propeller flew into the air. Flying over the slithering, splintering wreckage, I felt sure it had gone between my wings. When I looked round, I saw that the pilot of the Albatros had decided it was safer not to take any chances and had cleared off with Munro on his tail.

By this time, we were drawing close to Tsaritsyn and the Red fighters had decided that discretion was the better part of valour and hauled off. The other Camels appeared and began to circle, then, one after the other, everybody began to form up on me, with the DH9s at the back, and we flew home like that with everybody waving and grinning and mouthing questions at each other.

Puddy jumped from the cockpit as we landed and started to dance a jig. 'I gloat,' he yelled. 'I escape! Escape!'

He'd been running and walking south ever since he'd crashed and was half-starved and dehydrated when a lone Red cavalryman had finally found him. Spinning him a yarn about being the pilot of a Red scout which had been shot down, he'd managed to kill the horseman with his own sabre and had stolen his horse.

All the time he was talking, he was drinking champagne that Slingsby had found, and stuffing food into his mouth.

'I am never in danger,' he crowed. 'I am too clever for them.'

Gradually the celebration developed into a party that beggared description and everybody went mad. When everything was at its liveliest, there was a shout from outside the door and Munro put his head out. 'Hold it, hold it!' he yelled, turning to face us. 'There's a chap here says the Grand Duke Grigori has arrived to present Bratty with a decoration.'

There was immediate silence and Munro, who was standing in the doorway, began to talk to someone out of sight to the rest of us.

Then he slammed to attention and his arm clicked up in a salute that would have done the Grenadier Guards justice. We were all waiting, slightly awed, with me certainly wondering what the blazes was coming, when a man appeared in the doorway, clad in a Russian uniform with a Cossack hat. He wore a huge handlebar moustache and his jacket was studded with ribbons.

'Sir Major Bratty,' he announced. 'By order of General Wrangel, I present you with the order of St John of Jerusalem, St Pancras, St Alban's, St Mary-le-Bow, St Thomas's Hospital, St Leger, the Derby, the Oaks and the Grand National.'

He held out an aeroplane wheel, complete with spokes, hanging from a vast ribbon a foot wide that he'd found Heaven alone knew where. Behind him I could see Flight-Sergeant Merry and several of the flight mechs, who were also in on the joke, and as he hung it round my neck it dawned on me that under the face fungus it was Slingsby.

In the riot that followed, Munro thought about Olga and drew me aside. 'Hadn't we better tell her?' he said.

'What makes you think she doesn't know already?'

He looked round, puzzled.

'See Tommy anywhere?' I asked.

Olga arrived soon afterwards, in fact, radiant with happiness, to embrace her brother. Abramov had accompanied her but, after looking Puddy all over, he smiled at me. 'I think there is nothing he wants but food and rest,' he said. 'And perhaps a little something to drink.'

Olga was crooning over her brother, tears of happiness in her eyes, watched from behind by a beaming, benevolent Tommy looking like a great bear. Then, unexpectedly, she swung round and, kissing me with none of her usual reserve, she hugged me to her.

'*Oi Anglichanin*,' she said. 'You are so good to me!'

Tommy took out a large red handkerchief, blew his nose and, turning abruptly, disappeared outside.

The following morning we watched the hospital trains setting off for the south. One of them was thirty-three carriages in length and bandaged men stared from the windows with indifferent eyes. We gave them what cigarettes we had, all of us smoking ourselves because the stench as it passed us was appalling.

Train Number 643 was still down the line, however. Somehow, it seemed to have become attached to the Air Force and all our sick – most of them with cuts or sprained fingers – went there for treatment. Though Tommy was delighted it was staying, I wasn't so sure that it was wise; the night before I'd been over to the 47 Squadron train and heard that, though Wrangel was still hanging on to his positions in front of Saratov, he had little hope of capturing the town because on his right his allies were in retreat again. Begging for reinforcements or at least a change of orders, he'd been to see Denikin, convinced that, despite Denikin's nearness to Moscow, he could never reach it without a change of plan.

My worries must have shown in my face.

'What's up, sir?' Slingsby asked. 'You're brooding like Napoleon on the deck of the *Bellerophon*.'

I managed a smile. 'I'm just trying to get my ideas in order,' I said. 'In a straight line, the tallest on the right, the smallest on the left, all eyes right and threes about.'

'Perhaps if you keep quiet it'll go away,' he suggested.

'I don't think so,' I said, and told them what I'd heard.

'Masel', Ah dinnae think Denikin's got a chance,' Munro said. 'In fact, Ah think he's heading for a hell o' a defeat.'

Certainly the railway was beginning to be chaotic because, just as we'd been warned, Mahkno and his Greens had turned up in the area and were raiding depots and wrecking and looting trains. No one seemed able to stop them and the Whites even seemed to be losing control over the civilian population which had always been riddled with Red agents, while, with the peasants still crying out for land, there was little improvement in the relations between Denikin and the Cossack authorities.

Puddy was suddenly gloomy. He had quite recovered but was still convinced he'd cheated death only for it to appear again shortly in the future. 'We *seem* to be winning, Sir Major,' he said, 'but we are not really, I think.'

His words confirmed what Munro thought and what I'd felt myself for some time. 'Why do you say that, Puddy?' I asked.

He indicated a refugee train pushing past. It consisted of a long string of box cars, loaded with humanity which crammed the compartments, clung to the doors, crowded on the roofs and even huddled on little platforms built between the buffers.

'Do you think they would endure *that*,' he asked, 'if they were not afraid? Every time the train goes round a corner, someone always falls off. They are either killed or are left standing there in the middle of the steppe, miles from anywhere, while their relatives watch and wail as they grow smaller and the train draws away. You can always judge the situation by the behaviour of the refugees.'

'Are you sure, Puddy?'

He gave me a sad smile. 'I am an expert, Sir Major, I have been watching them since 1917.'

I realized he was right. The refugees *were* growing more alarmed and were crowding more and more urgently into every train that left, despite the shops and markets that were open in Tsaritsyn. Station officials were even making a very useful sideline by selling such things as hot water for washing or positions in the better coaches. The older ones, used again and again, were riddled with lice and fleas and everyone was terrified of being bitten and contracting typhus.

We were still flying while the weather remained good but there were days now when there were frosts in the morning and thick mists at night. The Red fighter pilots seemed to be merely watching now and rarely came up and I was suddenly reminded of Napoleon in 1812 and how the Russians had waited for the winter to destroy him. Could that be what they were doing now?

We lost Jasper with a bullet through his thigh and for some reason – I suspected sabotage *en route* – the message for a replacement never arrived and we had to manage with one pilot less.

And suddenly the typhus seemed to be spreading faster. One night we moved south unexpectedly, pulling back as Wrangel retreated to consolidate, and at one station we passed through there were fifteen bodies lying in a long row alongside the track waiting for burial. Behind them the walls of the station buildings, alongside the claptrap that the staff put out about the low morale of the Reds, were plastered with tragic little notices for people who'd become separated from their families.

'Piotr: Your family is in Novocherkassk.' 'Dear Masha, Look for us in Ekaterinodar.' 'Mikhail: Take the children to Tikhoretskaya. We will find you.'

Some of them were heartbreaking and, looking at the bodies left by relatives who dared not risk stopping, I began to see Russia as a vast indifferent plain full of people who were either weak and help-less, or cruel enough to prey on them.

Flight-Sergeant Merry reported that one of the flight mechanics was ill and a Russian doctor confirmed that it was typhus. Collishaw, who was worse, was to be sent to Novocherkassk so we took the opportunity to get rid of our own case. I had no wish to keep him with us because it was essential he had proper treatment, and the disease was only too quick to spread.

We had long ceased to take much notice of the Denikin communiqués which didn't even seem any longer to have a foot in the realms of reality. I don't know how we knew they were wrong but we did, and hearing that Cossacks were fighting with saboteurs in Tsaritsyn, we even began to wonder if Collishaw and the flight mechanic were safe.

I was aware that the feeling of oppression was growing. It wasn't fear, because I'd seen too much of war, but a sense of doom. For the first time I understood how Puddy's mind worked, though with him the sense of fatalism was personal, while with me it was collective and concerned a whole trainload of men and machines. In my heart I knew something was wrong and I was more than glad when Sykes appeared.

'Thought my place was here, not in Ekat,' he said, and I knew that he was also aware of the same feeling of impending disaster.

He brought news that the two sick men had passed safely through Tsaritsyn. 'Afraid they might have been taken off the train and shoved in hospital,' he said. 'Didn't want that. It's jammed with sick and wounded and all the trains going south are full of it, too.'

He was changed. Bleaker, somehow, and less communicative. He'd always enjoyed flying but for once he seemed indifferent and left me to run the flight while he moved between the A and B Flight trains, conferring with the De Havilland pilots. I struggled with Flight-Sergeant Merry to keep the Camels flying in deteriorating weather and I saw little of Sykes because, when he wasn't with the De Havilland crews, he was in the town, haunting the railway telegraph office where we picked up all our signals. Occasionally his old lazy charm showed through with that smile that could melt even the hardest heart, but for most of the time he was silent and kept to himself so that I wondered what he knew that I didn't. Two days after his arrival he told me.

He suggested a walk and as we moved alongside the track he explained.

'Government in London's got cold feet,' he said. 'Can't make up their mind. Half of 'em say we're not giving enough help, t'others say we're giving too much. Winston's still willing to continue intervention, but the Cabinet's voted for pulling out.'

'Pulling out?'

'That's the position. Orders are that all operational units – and that chiefly means us, Brat – are to leave. Only artillery instructors to remain behind. Not anxious, it seems, to be accused of trying to influence Russian politics.'

I knew there was something in the wind we didn't know about because Kolchak had just reoccupied Tobolsk and the Poles were advancing from the north-west, while Denikin was near Voronezh and Yudenich was said to be so near to Petrograd he could see St Isaac's Cathedral.

'They said he was near enough to chuck stones through the windows,' I said. 'Won't he get there now?'

Sykes shook his head. 'No.'

'Why not?'

'God knows. Because he's not wanted there. Because of the Russian character. And because this damned war was made by politicians who don't understand Russia.'

'I thought all that was wanted was one good push,' I said. 'And that then Lenin and all his pals would disappear.'

He shrugged. 'Far as I'm concerned, I don't give a damn' who runs Russia. Suppose, because of the way I was brought up. I hope the Whites'll win, but there's something to be said for t'other side, too, because there was a lot that was rotten in the old régime, and I'm not sure, anyway, that the Whites *will* win. Denikin's not the man for the job.'

I stared at him. For me the war in Russia had never been a crusade but I was still aware of the spirit that had sent me rushing to join the RFC to save Europe for civilization against the Germans in 1915. There was a lot of idealism in us all and it suddenly seemed to be turning sour.

When I tried to explain, Sykes gave me that sad slow smile of his. 'Not quite the same here, old son,' he said. 'And London knows it. All the same, a few strings have been pulled in Ekat and we've been allowed a choice. Wrangel wants us to stay. I shall put it to everybody tonight.'

We drew the flight up in a hollow square that evening and he told them the situation, standing on the steps of the mess car. Several of the mechanics who were married decided to go home. Munro, having already been given a posting, also didn't volunteer to stay, and I thought him wise. With his injured legs, he was best where he was safe because if things went wrong he might find his inability to walk far a great disadvantage. The rest preferred to stay with the flight. Since most of them were regulars, they'd long since discovered that service overseas – *anywhere overseas* – was always freer than service at home.

With the news things were suddenly not as easy as they had been. The insidious propaganda which was always being passed around among the civilians became more powerful and we always had to be on our guard against sabotage. In fact, 47 Squadron lost several box cars in a blaze and several of their mechanics received slight burns.

We strafed a column of Red cavalry trying to reach Tsaritsyn and bombed a train or two but the Reds seemed to have so many men now we didn't appear to be having much effect. Then we lost Stagg with a bullet through the cheeks of his bottom to leave a painful but not very serious wound.

'Four holes with one bullet,' Slingsby grinned. 'That's shooting, Staggy!'

Certainly the Reds were growing more experienced all the time and nowadays always seemed to be waiting for us when we went down. Finally one morning, when we woke, the steppe was white all over.

There'd been a cold drizzle for some time which was neither snow nor rain and that night the wind had got up, driving at the tethered machines and bending the saplings. There was a damp biting chill that heralded winter and a heavy grey sky, then the snow had begun to fall in wet feathery flakes, whirling down out of the darkness. After a while it had stopped but now here it was again, and the buildings and trains stood out against it with an iron blackness.

We managed to get off the ground, nevertheless, and the Red troops we were looking for were as sharp against the whiteness as if they were etched. One Spad came down out of the clouds to try to cut us off but he seemed to be a raging amateur and Slingsby shot off a wing so that it went floating away and the fuselage spun down to crash into the dark branches of a small wood like a shell exploding. Apart from this one machine the Red Air Force seemed to have disappeared.

By the time we returned, it had started to snow again, the flakes coming in stinging veils and freezing swathes to make flying a hardship in the icy prop blast. As we taxied in after landing I knew that we'd probably flown our last flight for that year; and that night the bottom dropped out of the thermometer and it was so cold you could hear the frost crackling under your boots as you walked along the train to where the mechanics were dismantling the machines with frozen fingers and packing them on the flat cars.

Olga was waiting in the mess car with Puddy and Abramov. She was wearing a fur coat and cap and she looked prettier than ever with her cheeks pink with the cold.

'I have come to say goodbye,' she announced.

Train Number 643 was finally leaving for the south, and she kissed me gently. 'Perhaps we meet in Ekat,' she said.

As she and Abramov rose to leave, Tommy arrived, red-faced with hurrying and with an expression full of disaster.

'I've just heard,' he said. 'They say you're leaving!'

Olga nodded and he gestured wildly. 'Ekat, isn't it?' he said. 'We've got to meet again some time! Will you write to me?'

She promised that she would but I noticed that as she left she only shook hands with him. He almost fell down the steps in his hurry to walk back with her.

Puddy turned to me, his handsome face appealing and twisted with anxiety. It was as if he knew the world was about to fall in on us. 'You will not change your mind, Sir Major?' he asked.

'No, Puddy,' I said. 'Try Tommy.'

'She do not want Tommy,' he announced.

'I'm sorry,' I said.

'Never mind.' He managed a smile. 'All will be well, of course. She is going to where it is safe and perhaps she will meet someone else.' He gestured and smiled again. 'Why should *I* worry about little Olga? It is *I* who will die. I have always known this.'

Chapter 7

We'd been aware for a long time that things were changing, and though Denikin took Orel and Novosil, within two hundred miles of Moscow – almost in the suburbs you could say – two days later, on 13 October, the Reds were near the Holy City of Kiev and it began to look as though they were going to cut off the heads of Denikin's armies from their bases.

We'd been expecting something of the sort for days because troop trains were already pulling out of Tsaritsyn and it was clear that the Saratov Front was beginning to crumble. Orders came up from Ekat that we were to withdraw with them, because Trotsky was battering at the junction of Sidorin's Army of the Don and Mai-Maievski's Volunteer Army. A week later there was more bad news. Despite the losses he'd suffered north of Tsaritsyn, Trotsky was hitting out with a tremendous numerical advantage in men, and had broken through the junction of Denikin's armies so that Denikin was having to evacuate Kursk and Orel in a hurry. He had spread his lines too thin and was now struggling to stop breakthroughs in half a dozen places at once because nowhere had he sufficient men to hold his Front.

The Reds weren't slow to take advantage of the disaster with propaganda and, while the Whites were novices at this kind of warfare, *they* were experts. Their pamphlets were everywhere, complete with maps to show how the Whites were retreating. With Kolchak drawing back, they were expecting Archangel to fall to them within weeks, while Yudenich was expected to be crushed beyond recovery at Petrograd and in the south Denikin would be driven into the sea. Victory was certain, they said. The Canadians had elected a Soviet and King George V was in the Tower of London, while President Wilson, of the United States, who had been elected in his place, was sleeping in Buckingham Palace. All the Whites could offer in reply were half-baked films showing badly equipped half-starved troops being reviewed by hosts of splendidly equipped and uniformed White generals, and posters indicating the tortures the Reds inflicted on prisoners. Since Red sympathizers in the cities were already handing out pamphlets telling the White soldiers it was safer to surrender, they didn't encourage anyone to fight to the last breath.

'I think,' Puddy said, 'that we shall need to pray on the relics of all the holy ones of Kiev for this benighted land of ours.'

With every Front falling apart, we were ordered to swing right across South Russia from east to west, right back where we'd started. There was nervousness in the air as we left and among the scented officers in the rear of the White Army there was suddenly a lot of bitterness towards us. From being the saviours of their cause the British were suddenly ingrates who were refusing to send them experienced divisions to help. Despite the mountains of British supplies, it seemed that the Russians, and the Russians alone, had been the architects of any White success there'd been. Even now, they hadn't grasped that the old days were over and they were still waiting for the miracle that would return their estates and wealth and privileges to them.

There was a marked uneasiness at the station as we waited for the train to be switched through, and the crowd surged up and down the platform as fear communicated itself from one to another. Someone slapped a fractious child and, as it screamed, the noise broke across the general sounds of mingled wretchedness.

The Russian regimental officers were watching their men with worried eyes, wondering if they were ready to turn on them. They were discussing quietly where the Reds might be, and whether their units contained Bolshevik agents, and I thanked God for the stolid British soldiers and mechanics at my back. I wouldn't have enjoyed commanding a Russian unit just then.

It was normally a seven-day trip to Debaltsevo but the refugees were beginning by now to swarm across every track. Many of them had journeyed in stages all the way from North Russia to escape Red vengeance and they were waiting at every siding, hoping for a southbound train, begging for a place on the cars or the flats, or even a handhold on the roof or the buffers. Many of them had old people with them, or infants in arms, and they were terrified and came at us in hundreds, pulling at our sleeves, old men and women kneeling in front of us, even to me who wasn't old enough to grow a decent moustache.

The news was all bad now. Kolchak was retreating from Omsk and Denikin's armies were in reverse on every Front except round Kharkov. In the north-east there had even been trouble with British Tank Corps men affected by Russian propaganda and one case of Russian troops murdering their British officers. It was even said that the Reds were butchering the population wherever we'd stopped our train and set up a headquarters.

Shuttling our train and the DH9s' trains behind us, Sykes' face was taut with worry, while Tommy, with no flying to occupy his mind, spent all his time wrapped in a blanket, trying with cold fingers to write lengthy letters to Olga without any real knowledge of where to address them. These days, Munro, trying to keep up our spirits with sing-songs, pounded the piano with an air of desperation. Permission for him to go home had come through but he was loath to up sticks, and preferred to remain with us at least as far as Tikhoretskaya where he could pick up another train for Ekat while we branched off north towards

Kharkov. It seemed, in fact, the only safe way to travel.

Near Rostov-on-Don, Wrangel's police were stopping every train, searching for stolen goods, loot and deserters. They didn't worry us much but we were held up by the trains ahead and were forty-eight hours late getting into the city. There was a signal from Mission headquarters calling Sykes down to Ekat but Munro, who could have gone with him, suddenly decided it was wiser to stay with us.

Because of the uncertainty and because we were trying to find a trainload of petrol, oil, spare parts and food, we went into the town – me and Puddy and Slingsby, leaving Munro in charge and Tommy with pen, ink and paper writing one of his hopeless letters to Olga. The place was already a confusion of White regiments and refugees. The bridge across the Don, an arched structure three hundred yards long, carrying a road and railway lines, which was the only means of crossing apart from ferries, was packed with vehicles and trains. The Borodinskaia, the main street, was thronged with people looking for food, transport or even relatives they'd lost, and those big war maps we'd seen when we'd first arrived were showing dwindling circles of red round Omsk, Kursk and Kharkov. But although buildings had been requisitioned for the troops the theatres were still open and there was even a choice of newspapers. And, despite the harrowing tales of wounded men crawling from the hospitals to the north rather than be left behind, there were still enough people weighed down with the wealth of generations to make it possible for the expensive restaurants to stay open. They didn't appear to care a fig for the men who were fighting to cover their retreat, men who had all too often lost their own families and homes and asked nothing more than to die in action in the hope of avenging them. Their wealth had always brought them privilege and they expected it to continue to do so.

We found the petrol, oil and spare parts – being offloaded by a squad of soldiers under a smart-looking captain in a fur coat, who looked as though he hadn't done too badly out of the war. Since there were several lorries full of trunks, cases and what looked like furniture waiting alongside, he obviously intended using the box cars for his loot.

I pulled out my revolver and stuck it under his nose. 'Tell him to put it all back, Puddy,' I said. 'Tell him if he doesn't I'll blow his stupid head off.'

The officer seemed startled. 'But the waggons are for General Guchkov!' he said.

'Who's General Guchkov?'

'Commissariat. He needs them for supplies.'

I gestured at the loot alongside. '*These* supplies, for instance?' I said.

He seemed to think there was nothing odd about removing my petrol, oil and food for General Guchkov's personal belongings, and we were deep in an argument when a colonel, equally well dressed, arrived and demanded to know what I was doing. When I told him, his face fell and he disappeared in a hurry. A few minutes later, the general himself appeared, a fat, white-haired man with a red nose that was veined with too much good living. He spoke French.

'Why are you stopping my men working?' he demanded.

'Because they are unloading my supplies,' I said.

The general made a sign and a moment later a squad of men marched round the end of the train and lined up facing us, their rifles at the ready.

'Puddy,' I hissed. 'Get back to the train and tell Flight-Sergeant Merry we need him and as many men as he can bring.'

As he disappeared, I turned to face the general. 'You're not having these waggons,' I said.

Slingsby, obviously quite enjoying the situation and quite prepared to give battle if necessary to the whole White Army, had also drawn his revolver, and as we stood with our backs to the train, Guchkov was in a dilemma because he knew as well as I did that if he tried to use force on us he'd be in trouble. For a long time we stood like that, Slingsby tormenting Guchkov with jeers, and arguments and entreaties breaking out, until, to my relief, because I wasn't sure what to do next, I saw Tommy, Puddy and two other officers appear, followed by Flight-Sergeant Merry and the biggest part of C Flight, all in full battle kit and armed with rifles.

Deciding he'd lost, Guchkov scowled heavily and stamped off through the snow with the colonel. The natty major was about to march his men off after them when I signed to Merry and he had them surrounded in no time.

'They reload the train first,' I said. 'Tell him, Puddy. Tommy, you stay here with a strong guard until we can arrange to shift it.'

–

By leaving an armed guard and lining up the rest of the squad outside the stationmaster's office, we got the supply train shunted to our own train. In the confusion it took us a whole twenty-four hours and, as we hitched it to the back of our own box cars, we saw troops moving south past the yard, long columns of men, guns, waggons and lorries, a sullen look about them all. Among them were Cossacks dragging bunches of Bolshevik prisoners on ropes, and if a prisoner slipped and fell, the horsemen didn't bother to stop, but simply hauled him through the frozen snow until he managed to stagger upright again, torn and bloody.

No one seemed to know anything and I kept a guard round the train all the time. I was growing sickened by this time of the sight of the crowded trains full of defeated men, while almost alongside them on the next track, indifferent to their feelings, Guchkov and his expensive-looking staff, with girls at their sides, dined in opulent coaches served by white-coated waiters, their tables covered with shining linen. It didn't make sense.

'Damn it,' I said furiously, 'don't they have *any* brains at all?'

The snow had fallen several times since we'd left the Tsaritsyn area and it was now thick underfoot. On every street corner, huge fires were blazing, surrounded by half-frozen soldiers, and the sky was like a grey blanket over the yard. It was as cold as charity now and my breath froze on the shaggy cap I wore, which Machikov, of Shkura's Wolves, had given to me as a souvenir during the summer. Uncertain what to do, I sent Slingsby into town to try to find out from Mission headquarters what was happening. He returned looking grey with cold.

'We've been told to wait,' he said. '*Peut-être*, we aren't going to Kharkov after all.'

-

The following day, to my relief, Sykes returned. He brought bad news:

'Lloyd George's saying in London that the British government considers the civil war in Russia over.'

'Och, charrmin',' Munro snorted. 'If yon doesna knock the ground from under oor feet, Ah dinnae ken what does.'

'I think this Lloyd George is a humbug,' Puddy observed.

'He probably thinks that Kharkov's a Russian general,' Slingsby agreed, 'and Wrangel's something you use to squeeze water out of washing.'

'During the war,' Munro said, 'they told us we were heroes and noble an' honourable because we were fightin' tae save the politicians and the profiteers from the Hun. Now that we're savin' 'em from the Bolshies they're tryin' to shove us under the carpet.'

'Didn't you know the wealthy and the selfish always survive, you juiceless old cynic,' Slingsby said. 'It's one of the facts of life – like sentimental young ladies needing manly breasts to weep on, or bully beef, or that if you fly Camels long enough the brain turns to solid fat.'

'We're naethin' but paid mercenaries lent by a conscienceless government tae a foreign power to fight in a squabble that's no' ours.'

Sykes shrugged. 'Which, in addition,' he said, 'is busy going the wrong way. Denikin's in a mess and there's a danger of his retreat becoming a rout. It looks less and less likely that we'll be allowed to go to Kharkov.'

'We could always go mad, of course,' Slingsby grinned, 'and retire gracefully to the coast, laden with decorations, honour, the spoils of war, and the gratitude of the Russians, to return home to the admiration of the great British sporting public, a garden party at Buckingham Palace and a knighthood for Bratty.'

'You've a hope, mon!' Munro said.

'I live in hope.'

'Well, this one's a forlorn hope, so you can forget it. They dinnae gie medals for defeats.'

–

We all knew that if we didn't reach Kharkov, the Reds might well capture the city, and if they did, the Whites' chief strategic base was lost, and we discussed the problems of keeping the aeroplanes flying in bad weather because, if it became any colder, they'd have to be drained of oil after every flight and the oil prevented from freezing with braziers.

'I think we're going to have to withdraw the DH9s,' Sykes said. 'And that's a pity because Wrangel could use them. He's supposed to be taking over Mai–Maievski's command, too. In the meantime, we'd better get as near to Kharkov as we can, just in case.'

It was easier said than done because the congestion at Taganrog held us up for half a day. There were few trains going our way now but the line was clear as far as Debaltsevo, then the trouble started again with a colossal jam in the marshalling yards. It was impossible to move north because every line was blocked with southbound trains which couldn't move and the stationmaster and his assistants had disappeared.

Then our own train crew decided they didn't want to go any further toward Bolshevik territory, and when we tried to contact British Mission headquarters at Taganrog, it was found the telegraph wires had been cut. In the end, Sykes told Merry to put a guard on the engine and if the crew tried to bolt to draw his revolver and start threatening them.

He sighed as Merry saluted and disappeared. 'They'll try, just the same,' he said. 'And it'll be impossible to watch 'em all the time. The situation's becoming impossible because we're going to be spending all our time looking over our shoulders.' He gave me a smile. 'Into the bargain,' he said, 'we're now in Mahkno's territory and, in addition to watching the Reds and our own train crews, we're going to have to keep a permanent guard alert in case he tries to attack us.'

We got out of Debaltsevo the following day. The heavily loaded engine began to move in fitful stops and starts, its wheels spinning on the icy track, then, as they began to grip, it jerked forward, moving faster and faster with a wild clatter of the wheels so that the ground trembled as it rumbled out of the town, scattering cinders and staining the snow as it went.

Even when we were clear of the yards movement remained slow, erratic and difficult. The south-bound trains, packed with terrified refugees, filled every junction and siding and sometimes it took hours of waiting while they shunted and backed so that we could pass on the north-bound line. Every stationmaster had to be bribed or threatened before we could move and it was always impossible to decide whether the reason was Bolshevik sympathy, inefficiency or sheer impossibility. We stopped, started and crawled, always able to get down from the train and walk about in the snow to stretch our legs because, even if the train left unexpectedly, it was so slow you could easily catch it up again.

It went on for two and a half days. 47 Squadron were just ahead of us but they were making no better time, and we all grew depressed at the sight of the streams of refugees and irritated with the impossibility of the situation. Christmas in Moscow was becoming nothing but a dream. With both tracks jammed with trains, each so close to the one in front they looked like one long train, as we waited in a siding for the way ahead to clear I suddenly realized that in all that vast caravan we were the only train heading towards the enemy.

With the chances of flying growing more hopeless every day in the white, fog-enshrouded landscape, Sykes decided to unload three of the machines and assemble them for take-off in case the weather broke and we could get into the air.

'We can keep the oil warm by wrapping tarpaulins round the engines and shoving paraffin stoves inside,' he said.

By this time, even the railway workers, who so far had regarded themselves as neutral and served both sides, were also beginning to desert and, into the bargain, the Greens were growing more active. Puddy tried hard to remain optimistic in spite of everything. 'Perhaps it is not so bad as it seems,' he said. 'After all, our cavalry have raided within a hundred and twenty miles of Moscow.'

'Aye, mebbe,' Munro growled, 'but the Whites have started tae desert in droves.'

Puddy persisted, but it was difficult because it was obvious the Whites were running out of funds, arms and equipment, and their armies were still hampered by the hopeless inefficiency of the old regime, Cossack separatism, corruption and Denikin's policies and strategies; to say nothing of French desertion, British half-heartedness and American uncertainty.

—

The trains that had passed us heading south had contained refugees with a sprinkling of wounded. But now, as we unloaded the machines, we noticed that the soldiers weren't always wounded. The following day, the sprinkling increased to a fair number and by the third day the trains were packed with troops, infantry and cavalry, packed solid inside and out despite the cold, squatting on the tops of the coaches, clinging to the steps, or huddling over the buffers. They were all white from the intermittent snowfalls and a lot of them were drunk.

They told us Kursk had fallen but, at that moment, we were far more concerned with keeping warm. None of us had furs but it wasn't hard to buy them from the refugees. Some of the wealthy ones had more than they needed and we didn't hesitate to barter food for them until every man was wearing a fur cap and a warm coat and great felt boots. We also looted a couple of pot-bellied stoves from a village nearby. One we installed in the officers' mess and the other in one of the *terplushkas* for the men, and we kept them red-hot with logs from alongside the track.

Even the Cossacks, who'd always been ardent supporters of the Whites in the hope that it would bring them their independence from Moscow, were beginning to slip away now to their homes, and one night we saw groups of them moving south, crossing the track on their shaggy ponies.

The moon was up and the snow dazzling white and hard enough for the horses to tread on without their feet sinking in. A nagging breeze plucked at their clothes, and their faces were tired and strained. The horses' heads hung with weariness and every man rode in his own little cloud of pale smoke where his breath and the breath of his horse hung in the air.

They told us that Wrangel had taken over Mai-Maievski's command at last but there were no orders for us; and Kinkead, of 47 Squadron, arrived in a fury because someone had stolen their engine during the night and they needed to find another. The following day the traffic south suddenly stopped, and I knew it meant that somewhere to the north the Bolsheviks had got across the track. There would be no more trains to the coast, and up ahead the occupants of the stranded trains were being murdered alongside the track.

We all knew what it meant. We'd reached the end. We could go no further forward. From now on the only way we could go was back.

'I think we'd better find out what we can,' Sykes decided, and Slingsby and I took off. The whole countryside was white – brilliant white in an unexpected sun – so white it dazzled and, because it reflected the clear sky, the distance seemed to disappear so that at times it was like flying in a cloud without a horizon.

We deliberately remained low to draw fire, knowing that shots would at least show where the enemy was, and sure enough we were soon able to identify Budenny's cavalry. As the machine-guns opened up on us, we pinpointed the enemy lines to the north of Debaltsevo and could see quite clearly the White Armies falling back before them.

With no engine to haul them back, 47 Squadron were beginning to grow worried and had broken out all their rifles, prepared to fight for it if they were stranded. We were just discussing ways and means of cramming them in with us and whether we should burn their machines, when Sykes managed to get in touch with General Holman at the British Mission, who arrived soon afterwards with a single engine and tender. He made no attempt to hide the situation from us. After six months of success, the White Armies were being dogged by disasters and the Reds were expected in Kharkov within a matter of days, while only a miracle could prevent them taking Kiev. Mai-Maievski had already disappeared and only Wrangel could prevent disaster. To give time for 47 to pull out behind Holman's engine, we were asked to destroy the track behind us.

We flew at tree-top height along the line and dropped our bombs bang on the points. How much damage we did was hard to say because there were plenty of horsemen about who took the opportunity to shoot at us, but, circling back, I saw the craters were all where they should be and knew we'd gained a few precious hours. To repair the points, the Bolsheviks would have to rip up other track further north, and that would take time.

The same evening we reloaded the Camels on the flats and started south, standing on the rear platform of the last car to watch the long straight track behind us dwindling like a black arrow in the white vastness of the plain. The next day, with Sykes ahead of us trying to clear a passage for us, we had our first attack from a band of Greens.

They arrived just after dark and our first intimation of their presence was the arrival of one of the crew of the machine-gun we'd posted on the platform at the end of the mess car. He almost fell into the saloon, yelling.

'Sir! Major! They've come!'

Crowding to the windows, we could see them in the distance across the snow, riding the shaggy mud-plastered Siberian transport ponies that everyone was now using as cavalry horses, dark figures drawing closer to the train as it thundered along. Then a flare went up and, as the whole scene was illuminated, the first crackling burst of firing made us duck our heads.

'Get that gun going,' I yelled to the machine-gunners and as it began to roar I saw a bunch of riders scatter, leaving two or three of their number on the ground.

Sending Slingsby swinging from the car along the train to make sure everyone was alert, we broke out the rifles and waited for the next attack. Fortunately, the captured Very lights the Greens were firing enabled us to see them better than they saw us and, with piles of cartridges stripped from machine-gun belts, we started shooting back from the windows as they appeared over the brows of low hills or from behind bunches of snow-clad trees.

The raid didn't last long because the Greens always reckoned that if they couldn't capture a train in twenty minutes it was best to break off the fight. They didn't hit anyone but the sides of the coaches were badly splintered. The refugee trains, less well armed, hadn't all held them off and we passed several burned-out wrecks by the track, with scattered corpses in the snow alongside.

We were down to bully beef and biscuits by this time and the chances of picking up anything else were pretty slender because we were right at the rear of a long line of trains heading south and wherever we stopped had been picked clean long before we arrived. We were making no more than ten miles a day now but, by bribing with canned food, we managed to persuade a railway official to shunt us ahead. Nobody was going to benefit from our skill if we were left behind, and we felt no qualms of conscience, because with both up and down lines crammed with trains now, we could only move forward when the train ahead of us moved. Every time we stopped, the train behind us stopped within a yard of our rear buffers, and whenever an engine broke down, as they often did, everybody swarmed off it and, with tree trunks and railway jacks, pushed it off the tracks. If it were possible, the coaches were attached to the train in front. If that were already too heavily laden, the coaches went over, too, and the passengers crammed themselves somehow aboard the next train or the one ahead. Since it took hours to do the job, whenever it happened the whole line of trains came to a stop until the track was clear.

The typhus had reached epidemic proportions by now and the refugees were dying in hundreds; with conditions fast becoming nightmarish every station had a line of frozen bodies lying on the platform, left there because the ground was too hard to open. Sometimes they belonged to children crushed to death in the scramble to board trains, but more often they were typhus victims. Every building displayed red-lettered notices insisting on precautions against the disease and pointing out that everyone should wash and clean their clothes. But, as there was no fuel to heat water and every tap was frozen, they were all quite pointless, and nobody changed their clothing because most of the refugees had no change of clothing anyway, and they were so packed in their compartments it would have been valueless.

Occasionally, a weeping relative stayed behind to mourn the dead but more often they merely dried their eyes and accepted that there was nothing they could do and left them there. With our inoculations and the possession of a service medicine chest, we had so far had only one case and it was just as well, because when we reached Taganrog, the hospital was a bedlam with an enormous line of stretchers waiting in the snow outside until someone inside died or recovered.

In the prevailing gloom there was one small gleam of light. Train Number 643 had turned up again. They had been to Ekat to unload and been sent north again to pick up more patients, and occasionally Abramov and one or two of the nurses appeared to share the hot toddy we made with service rum. I did my best to keep out of the way, unable to face Olga's misty-eyed looks and Puddy's appealing glances, but Tommy was in a seventh heaven. Once Munro appeared in my compartment.

'She's asking where y'are, mon,' he said. 'Are ye no' comin' oot?'

I put down the novel I was reading. 'Tell her I'm sick,' I said. 'No, better not say that or she'll be in here wanting to cure me. Tell her I'm working.'

'Mon, mon, it looks damned rude!'

I shrugged. 'These are rude times, Jock,' I said. 'And I'm not getting involved. Leave it to Tommy. He won't complain.'

By this time, the weather was bitter, the hoar frost like a thick fur over everything. The streets were covered with black ice and horsemen had taken to wrapping their feet in sacking to avoid frostbite. Every window was covered with a crust of frozen snow, and *droshkies* had been replaced by sledges. Guards in the yards chafed their hands and stamped their feet while men with crowbars worked over the points. Engines sighed and clanked and occasionally a train moved off, watched enviously by those with no place on it. More rarely, a hospital train or a general's equipage passed through on an open line, the windows opaque with frost, while figures trudged past, their heads down in their collars, black against the leaden sky.

The Russians were muffling themselves up in anything that came to hand, even stuffing straw under their shirts, and the rivers had become sluggish, with slabs of ice forming along the banks before breaking away and swirling in the current. As the water congealed again, they came to a stop once more and the ice built up against them in angular shapes, so thick now horses and even guns could cross it. But with the ice all the defensive lines the Whites had built up along the rivers had gone and there was no longer a barrier against the Reds.

Everyone was aware of the danger and every now and then a horseman arrived in a wild gallop with a message to bring his mount to a slithering stop, or a car would dash past, full of grim-faced officers. Headquarters was a waste of torn paper as documents were destroyed and the traffic jam had become so colossal those refugees who had money were beginning to leave the trains and buy sledges or carts or ponies and head south on their own. A long black string of struggling figures already stretched away ahead alongside the track, starving horses and oxen pulling sledges and carts, people on foot carrying everything they possessed on their person, in suitcases, perambulators or in sandbags. Vast groups of them kept besieging us, begging to be taken along with us, many of them with fever-stricken children. But our orders were strict. We were not to get involved and it was heartbreaking to have to refuse.

Tommy, his eyes agonized, stood on the step pushing them back. '*Nye refuganski poyezd*,' he kept saying. 'It's not a refugee train.'

As we moved forward they changed their minds and made a mad rush for the train in front or the train behind and the fight to get aboard started. Immediately children were left behind or pushed aboard by parents who found that they themselves could not then climb the steps for the crush.

The knowledge that it was finally all over came when Sykes reappeared. The day was full of blanketing snow, grinding frost and mist, with the sun hanging among the winter-blackened trees, its light coming through only in weak amber rays. The icicles hanging from Sykes' fur cap tinkled like the crystals of a chandelier and his clothes were covered with frost rime. He looked exhausted as he grasped eagerly at the mug of hot rum we offered.

'The Reds have taken Poltava, Novonikolayevka and Kiev,' he said. 'Kolchak's armies are in ruins and nothing in the world can stop the Reds driving Denikin's forces apart. If that happens, heaven help us.'

He took a sip of the rum and sighed. 'Denikin's still clinging to his "Russia, One and Indivisible",' he went on. 'Wrangel's a bit more realistic. He wants to give up Rostov.'

'Ah hope he doesnae gie it up just yet,' Munro said grimly. 'We've got to cross the Don there.'

'Denikin's promised he won't abandon his Front without giving us time to get clear,' Sykes said. 'Unfortunately, it seems to me that he's no longer got much control over the situation.'

Nobody spoke. There was nothing to say. Ahead of us everything was collapsing into confusion and behind us was only the darkness of anonymity.

–

The following morning there was a raid on the train by refugees determined to climb aboard. For a quarter of an hour we pushed them off, and when we'd finished we found Puddy sitting by the track holding his ankle, his face twisted in agony.

'What happened?' I demanded.

'I slip on the step as I climb in,' he said. 'By all the saints in the calendar, it hurts!'

We carried him to Train Number 643 where Dr Abramov said that the ankle was broken.

Puddy beamed. 'Then I can stay here?' he asked. 'With my little sister?'

Abramov shrugged but Olga pleaded for her brother and a bunk was found for him on condition that as soon as he could he'd leave. 'Cheerio, old son,' Slingsby said. 'Just make sure you keep your revs up. Bon vwayage.'

We left all the magazines we possessed, together with a bottle of slivovitz to keep him happy, and headed back to our own train to find Flight-Sergeant Merry with a long face.

'Now what?' Sykes asked.

'One of the mechanics, sir,' he said. 'He's complaining of headaches and a few other things. It looks to me like another case of typhus.'

Within twenty-four hours the sick man was vomiting and shuddering with chill. Twelve hours later he was delirious and sweating in his bunk, his face bloodless, his mouth shouting fragments of memories from the war in France. Because lice swarmed in the woodwork of the neglected rolling stock the disease was spreading like wildfire and whole truckloads of people were dying untended or were frozen to death because they were too weak to help themselves. Despite the precautions we took and the disinfectant and flea-repellants we used, it was a miracle more of us hadn't caught it.

Dr Abramov was in no doubt what should be done. 'He should be isolated,' he said.

By this time the sick man's body was covered with red blotches and we knew his condition was serious, so we kept him separate at the end of the train and just hoped we could look after him. Sykes was clearly worried and Munro was suddenly depressed and complaining of a headache. 'Ah'm no masel',' he said. 'Mebbe Ah'm homesick or somethin'.'

But that evening he couldn't eat anything and during the night I heard noises coming from his compartment and went out to find Slingsby holding him while he vomited his heart up. His face was grey, there were tears in his eyes and he was shuddering with cold.

'For God's sake, Jock,' I said. 'You ought to be in bed.'

We bullied him back between the sheets and, leaving Slingsby sitting by the bed, bathing the sweat off his forehead, I roused Sykes.

'I think Munro's got *tif*,' I said.

We had no means of looking after two sick men for long and we went in search of Train Number 643 again. The town was chaotic now and the hotel where we'd eaten and drunk on our last visit had been wrecked. It looked as if the whole town had rampaged through it. Windows were smashed, much of the furniture had disappeared and mud and snow had been tramped among the overturned plants and smashed glass. There was no staff beyond two flashily-dressed maids who didn't attempt to hide their delight at the imminent arrival of the Bolsheviks.

As we left we bumped into Dr Abramov. He looked tired but he didn't hesitate. 'Of course I will take your Officer Munro,' he said 'Bring him along. We are leaving in twenty-four hours and we have priority. We will give him every moment of our time that we can.'

Munro was incoherent as we loaded him on a stretcher, and was talking about things that only he knew about. Some of them I recognized – 'Bull,' he kept yelling. 'There's one behind you! There's one behind you!' The tell-tale blotches were all over his body now, and in a rare moment of sanity he managed to speak to me through white lips.

'Och, mon,' he moaned. 'Tae think Ah survived all yon crashes for this!'

Four mechanics carried him to the hospital train. Inevitably Tommy managed to attach himself to the party.

Puddy was waiting in the mess car. 'I am happy to give up my bunk for Officer Jock,' he said. 'Is a very comfortable one, I promise.'

Olga and Abramov saw Munro to his bunk then returned to say goodbye.

'*Do svidaniya*,' Olga said hopelessly. 'It is a world of goodbyes.'

She seemed to sense that I was holding her at arm's length, and, aware of Tommy watching with miserable eyes, I kissed her and then Tommy kissed her, too.

When we returned to the flight train mail had appeared and there was a letter for Munro. Since he was unconscious, Sykes had opened it in case it contained anything important. It was from Barbara Hatherley, begging him to hurry home, because she was hoping to be married in the spring. There was also one from Charley and underneath the usual banter I detected a thread of anxiety.

'I hear some funny stories coming out of Russia,' she wrote. 'If anything happens to you, I shall want to know why, because this isn't at all what I expected.'

It wasn't what I'd expected either, I thought.

Chapter 8

When we left Taganrog the next day, half a dozen *terplushkas* loaded with refugees had been hitched behind us.

'Damn the orders,' Sykes had said. 'They can't be left behind to be butchered by Budenny's cavalry.'

It was the children that defeated us. Big-eyed, uncomplaining and utterly bewildered, they watched silently as their parents argued and pleaded, and even Slingsby's sleight of hand that produced titbits from our larder from behind their ears didn't bring much response. I think they were so hungry and exhausted nothing meant much to them any more. There had been fighting in and around the trains in the yards the night before, when Bolshevik sympathizers had tried to throw the place into confusion to make its capture easier for the Red cavalry, and in the dark it had been difficult to tell who was refugee and who was the enemy, because the attackers were all wearing civilian clothes.

The journey to Rostov was as bad as, if not worse than, the journey to Taganrog. There was a two-line track, with nothing going north and only headquarters and hospital trains allowed south on the up track. Guards were posted on the engines in case desperate refugees sheltering in abandoned coaches should steal them and hitch them to their own train. Everywhere there were overturned engines forced from the track with their box cars and coaches, most of them inhabited by desperate people trying to keep warm and by the criminals who were preying on them.

'I'm cold,' Slingsby announced. 'In fact, I'm beginning to feel damned uncharitable towards the Russians.'

'It's like measles,' someone said. 'It'll pass.'

'Not with me. Like wooden legs, measles runs in my family. But intrepid birdmen aren't supposed to be frozen by their feet to the ground.'

'You'll get over it.'

'Not me, old tin of fruit. I've never been as brave as the politicians in their cosy little offices who think these jolly little jaunts up for us.'

As we neared the coast, the Sea of Azov appeared on our right, cold and grey and shrouded with the mist that rolled across the bay from the Black Sea. The road alongside the track was crammed with an endless line of people, both civilians and soldiers, the civilians all walking because the soldiers had stolen their waggons and sledges and horses. The typhus was hitting them all and there were bodies alongside the road, most of them stripped of their clothing which had been donned by half-frozen people who'd become indifferent to the risk of typhus in their desperate attempts to keep warm.

It was near a place called Chelyinsk that we found the water tanks that refuelled the engine frozen solid, and we turned everybody out, military and refugees alike, to fill the engine with snow. Since snow melts into a very small amount of water, it took hours; and while everybody was hard at it, Tommy and I struggled along the track to look for Train 643 and see how Puddy and Munro were.

The train had been shunted ahead, however, by-passing others in an attempt to get the sick and wounded south, and there was no sign of it so that we returned faintly depressed, aware that it was impossible to do anything now but cross our fingers and hope for the best.

While we were talking, Slingsby touched my shoulder.

'Take a look at this, *mon brave*,' he said, and, peering through the frost-rimed windows, I saw another train moving past us. Officers covered with braid stared back at us through the windows.

'Staff train.' Sykes had joined us and was staring with us. 'Taganrog's being evacuated after all.'

'So much for Denikin's promise that he'd wait until we were clear.'

Another carriage slid into view and, eating in a clean, well-furnished dining car whose windows were partly steamed up with the heat inside, was the same General Guchkov who'd tried to steal our supply train on the way north.

Tucker frowned and shivered. 'Do you know what day it is?' he asked. 'It's Christmas Eve.'

Time had shot past so quickly we'd forgotten all about Christmas but, in any case, there wasn't much to celebrate with and none of us were in the mood, anyway. Several children among the refugees at the back of the train were sick with typhus and unlikely to live, and always, with monotonous regularity, there was that long line of desperate people tramping through the snow alongside. The cook made up a broth of bully beef and we handed it round next day in place of Christmas dinner.

'I'm a fairly easy-going chap,' Slingsby said darkly, 'but I'm beginning to have bad feelings about bully beef.'

It was as well we'd provided food because the engine driver and his mate had decided they'd have to leave to look after their families, and only the fact that we could still produce a hot broth changed their minds.

We didn't keep them for long, though, because the next night General Guchkov found his engine frozen up and sent men back along the line who uncoupled our engine and stole it with its crew. By bribery or threats of shooting, they'd managed to clear the up track and, like 47 Squadron not long before, we were left standing in the middle of dozens of refugee trains unable to move.

I'd never seen Sykes so angry. His face was taut and thin-looking and his eyes glittered like ice. 'Turn out the men, Brat,' he ordered. 'I'm going to get that damned engine back! So let's have an armed guard round the flats and box cars in case anybody tries to turn them over.'

While Tommy and the others lined the sides of the train with rifles and machine-guns, Sykes and I trudged along the track to see what we could find. Up ahead, we found Hospital Train 643 and climbed aboard as we passed to see how our sick were.

Puddy was living in the mess car now with his splinted leg on a chair. At night he slept on the floor and, apart from a firm conviction even now that death was waiting just round the corner for him, he looked as though he were recovering. 'All hospital trains have been cleared to Rostov,' he said. 'Perhaps there I shall be recovered and able to rejoin you.'

He was under no obligation to stay with us, but unlike many of his class in Russia, he had a strong sense of duty and, since his conviction that he was going to die was very real, he seemed to think it pointless trying to save himself.

The flight mechanic had died and Munro was unconscious but with his eyes open. He looked ghastly, his lashes gummed up, his lips cracked and sore and his teeth discoloured, and as I turned to Abramov he lifted his shoulders in a gigantic shrug.

'I don't know,' he said wearily in answer to my unspoken question. 'We are due to move out tonight and if we can only reach Rostov I think he will be all right. They're preparing to hold the bridge until we're all across the river. After that we shall be safe.'

There was nothing we could do. I left Munro's letters with Puddy, with instructions to pass them on if he recovered enough to read them, and went in search of Olga. Like Abramov she looked exhausted, thin-faced and feverish-eyed.

'We have *tif* aboard,' she said. 'Not just the patients. Some of the staff have it too, now. We've already lost Dr Oklov.'

Never in my life had I felt so helpless. As her eyes filled with tears and a vast sob burst from her, I put my arms around her and let her cry on my chest. For a minute or two she didn't move then she seemed to get control of herself and pushed me away. Looking up, she blinked away the tears and I handed her my handkerchief to dry her eyes. It wasn't very clean – we'd long since had to give up washing because of the lack of water – but she accepted it without a word.

We drank a glass of tea with them, while other nurses appeared, all of them as tired as Olga was, and as we rose to go she put her arms round my neck and clung to me, so that I had to unclasp her fingers and push her gently away. Her eyes were tragic and I had an uncomfortable feeling that she'd decided I was going to die and was trying to fix in her mind how I looked.

We climbed down and stood in the snow along-side as the train moved off, with Puddy clinging to the steps waving back at us. We watched the blank bare end of the last coach as it vanished from sight, then moved on again past huddled groups of people by the roadside, crouching round fires they'd built. Most of them wouldn't survive, I knew. One mother was sitting alongside her children who lay quite dead under a rug. She looked demented but nobody bothered to comfort her. There were too many around her in the same condition and in that appalling catastrophe everyone had lost all feelings of sympathy.

Yet none of them complained. It was almost as if they knew they were going to die but were hanging on to what few shreds of strength they had left so that they might struggle on a little further and at least avoid the sabres of the Red cavalry. A few even kept trying to climb aboard the halted refugee trains, only to be kicked off the steps with cries of 'Full up!', and at the station hundreds more were crammed into the waiting room trying to get near the stove in the hope of just a little warmth.

There had been looting in Chelyinsk and the windows of empty houses had been shattered and doors broken down. Furniture had been dragged out and burned for warmth; and the streets were full of household articles – curtains, chairs, pots, pans, books, clothes. Occasional corpses lay in corners, sometimes dead of typhus or smallpox, occasionally with blood on them to show they'd been murdered for what they possessed. Snow-plastered lorries growled through the streets, every one of them with its own little group of refugees alongside begging to be taken along.

In the station yard there was a single engine and tender getting steam up, complete with crew and stationmaster.

'I want this engine,' Sykes said.

'*Nyet.*' The stationmaster's hands waved in refusal. 'Is not possible. Is all ready to go.'

'Where?'

The stationmaster pointed and Sykes grabbed his arm. 'On its own?'

There was a long three-sided argument in halting Russian and halting English, and as it progressed, it occurred to me that the driver could understand more than he pretended. I drew him on one side and a little later I touched Sykes' arm.

'The driver says that it's to be attached to General Guchkov's train,' I pointed out.

'He's got *one* engine,' Sykes snapped. 'Ours! Right, get aboard!' He yanked out his revolver and forced the stationmaster aboard, too. The driver and fireman seemed to welcome the change of owner-ship and even began to smile.

The stationmaster begged and shouted and waved his arms but Sykes kept the snout of his revolver thrust up under his chin so that there was nothing he could do. At every set of points on the way back I climbed down with him and made him change the track until eventually, just as darkness was coming, we backed the tender up against our own train. The fitters and riggers were standing alongside smoking and, when it dawned on them that the engine was for them, they burst into cheers.

I jumped down and got hold of Merry and Slingsby. As they climbed, complete with revolvers, into the cab with the stationmaster, Sykes told them what was wanted.

'It's your job to see that he doesn't get away,' he said. 'If he does I'll probably shoot you instead.'

We left them to it and within half an hour the train jerked. The refugees standing alongside the rear *terplushkas* began to scramble aboard, plus a few who hadn't been on board before. An hour later we were clear of the town and on the down line heading for Rostov. There we learned that Likhaya, seventy-five miles to the north, had fallen, and the Reds were now advancing on Novocherkassk with nothing to stop them. If Novocherkassk fell they could well be into Rostov ahead of us and I thanked God that the hospital train had got away ahead of us. By this time, it could only be well down the line and probably even over Rostov Bridge, into the lonely countryside of the Kuban and on its way to Ekaterinodar and the coast.

I hoped it was *well* on its way, because we'd heard that the Kuban troops were now wanting to throw in their hands and go home. Denikin and Wrangel were still at each other's throats and Wrangel, in fact, had thrown up his command and left to form a ring of troops round Novorossiisk for when the military trains arrived. If the White troops were to be taken off in ships with their families, the Reds had to be held north of the city.

For a whole day we made good time, then suddenly the move southwards came to a stop again in the usual endless column of refugee trains. Alongside us grim-faced Cossacks pushed through the long trail of refugees beside the track, huddled in their coats, their caps covered with snow, dragging carts containing their wounded and sick. The typhus epidemic had reached fantastic proportions now because everyone was exhausted and under-nourished and a perfect prey to germs. Every station had its log-like figures of the dead.

It didn't seem possible that it could grow any more bitter, but it did. It was even painful to breathe because the air was like icicles in your throat and nostrils and in every village huge fires burned in the streets. Sometimes the whole village had gone up in flames. With many of the windows of our coaches shot out by the Greens and with fuel for the stoves now impossible to find, we were stiff with cold and praying either for the journey to end or the weather to break.

By this time, many of the railway workers were making no bones about their political sympathies, and were sullenly refusing to help. Remembering General Guchkov, I felt I couldn't blame them.

One hour of anguish followed another before we got going again, then, just north of Rostov, we were held up once more by sporadic shooting and another colossal traffic jam. Because the ground was too frozen to dig trenches, White troops were building barricades of snow cemented to iron hardness with water that had turned to ice.

Eventually we spotted the bridge across the Don, and soon afterwards we came into the Rostov yards. The river beyond the snow-covered bluffs was frozen in a moonscape of lumps and ridges, a dredger held fast in it like a fly in amber, and every field alongside was covered with a solid coating of ice where it had overflowed. There was an ominous quiet in the town. No one was under any delusions but that the place was going to fall to the Bolsheviks. It was quite obvious that the White Army was too confused to hold anything. Defeat had been brought about by lack of organization, selfish generals, corruption, laziness, indifference and that curious inability of old régime officers to react swiftly to events. All those recruits who'd been swept into the White armies during the summer had vanished, changing sides as quickly as they could, and the bodies of deserters who'd been caught hung from the lamp posts, the snow in the folds of their clothing. The Bolsheviks were only just to the north and, though the number of White troops passing through the place discouraged them from attacking, they already had machine-guns trained on the bridge and were trying to bring traffic to a halt.

Leaving Slingsby in charge of the train, Sykes and I went into the town, Sykes to find the British Mission for orders, me to collect mail and messages. The town was quiet under the snow. Shops were boarded up and houses silent, the streets empty except for occasional squads of marching men or an exhausted troop of cavalry slumped in their saddles. Down by the river a trickle of refugees was beginning to make its way across the ice, and the industrial areas on the right bank of the Don – the paper mills, distilleries and shipyards – seemed to reflect their black shapes.

There was nothing for us at the station, but the British signallers running the telegraph office told me that the station staff were leaving. From them I also learned that Train 643 had been ordered to discharge its sick and wounded into the hospital and been sent six miles back up the line to collect a new load.

'For God's sake,' I thought. 'Jock and Puddy!'

The hospital was crammed with sick and wounded and there was an air of paralysed, unspoken terror about it so that remarkably little was being done. I found Puddy sitting in a wheelchair by an open window.

'There is much typhus,' he explained gaily. 'But I have notice that fresh air is best, so I sit here. I shall remain free of the *tif*, I think, but perhaps I catch pneumonia instead.'

'We'll come and get you before we leave,' I promised. 'What about Munro?'

He gave a beaming smile. 'Officer Jock was long ago placed by British Mission officers aboard a fast train south. He was already recovering.'

As I left I saw that the trickle of refugees down to the river had suddenly become a horde and that the streets were packed with people. Where they'd all come from in a matter of an hour or two I couldn't imagine but only some disastrous news could have dragged them from the holes and corners where they were sheltering and set them on the move again.

I met Sykes in the Borodinskaia and told him about Munro. 'He ought to be in Ekat by now,' I said.

'Thank God for that,' Sykes said. 'Because, from now on, any moving of trains is going to depend on the passengers themselves. The last of the railway staff's cleared out.' He gave me a tired smile and showed me a Red Army communiqué he'd found. 'God knows where they come from,' he said. 'But everybody seems to have them.'

The news it contained was horrifying enough. The Donets coal basin was in the hands of the Bolsheviks who had cut Denikin's armies clean in half and were now hammering at the gates of Tsaritsyn, while Kolchak's forces were throwing down their arms in thousands. The fall of Taganrog and Rostov was expected within days.

Sykes had obtained places for us on a Mission train which was waiting in the yards to cross the bridge and there was no time to waste.

'All aircraft, ammunition and bombs are to be destroyed,' he said. 'White units are holding the Bolshies back north of the town until all the military trains have crossed and their engineers are already planting explosives on the bridge. But they can't hang on long and the Reds are already trying to infiltrate saboteurs to destroy it before everybody's across and they're bringing an icebreaker down so there'll be no escape across the ice.' His face was grim. 'Things are bad, Brat. They're even leaving the wounded behind, so you'd better go and get Puddy.'

I pushed my way down the Borodinskaia between the two human currents suddenly surging up and down its slushy surface, the riff-raff of a broken army and all the wreckage of a population it had dragged along with it in its retreat. All about me I could hear the crash of glass or the splintering of wood as White soldiers broke into houses to find a strip of red material to stick in their caps to bring immunity when the Reds arrived.

When I reached the hospital again, it was clear they'd received orders to evacuate, too, and the place was in a panic. Doctors and nurses were struggling to get wounded men into cars, lorries, vans and waggons that they'd mustered from nowhere; and Puddy had disappeared from his place by the window. In desperation I went through the place from top to bottom but it was a shambles, with the dead among the sick and wounded and everybody shouting to everybody else to hurry but nobody in charge to organize anything.

There was no sign of Puddy and, with the records in confusion, no one had even heard of him. Sick at heart, I made my way back to the train. When I arrived every man in the flight was waiting alongside with what kit he could carry. I sorted out my own kit in a matter of minutes and when I climbed down to the track again, everyone had piled their equipment and weapons, and armed sentries were standing over them.

Sending Tommy off to find a route to the Mission train, Sykes got the men scattering petrol over the aeroplanes and whatever was left. As I watched, they detached the box cars containing the refugees and made their occupants push them a safe distance away. The last of our stocks of clothing were handed over to them, together with anything else they fancied and what was left of the bully beef and biscuits. Since we'd been living hand-to-mouth ourselves, there wasn't much. As they stood by, watching with bewildered faces, the men formed up again with their rifles, equipment and full pouches. Vickers and Lewis guns were carried by their crews.

As they pushed the refugees back, Flight-Sergeant Merry stepped forward with a Very pistol.

'Go ahead, Flight,' Sykes said.

Merry pushed a cartridge into the pistol and aimed it. As he did so, he looked round, as if finding it hard to believe we were destroying everything we possessed.

'Go on, Flight,' Sykes snapped. 'Fire the damn thing!'

Merry drew a deep breath and pulled the trigger. The flare struck the wing of the nearest Camel, to lie burning in the angle formed by the wings and fuselage. The fabric started to flare, then there was a tremendous 'whoof' as the scattered petrol caught, and one after the other the Camels went up in roaring flames and coiling smoke. Then the flat cars caught, followed by the box cars, and in seconds the whole train was burning.

There was no point in standing around waiting.

'Form 'em up, Flight,' Sykes said, and Merry got the men into columns of fours. Finding one of the refugees who could speak a little English, Sykes explained what was in the burning cars and warned him to keep everyone well clear, but as we moved off I looked back and saw the crowd already edging nearer with the clear intention of climbing into the burning cars to salvage what they could.

We hadn't gone more than a few hundred yards when the first of the bombs went off, then there was a colossal explosion that seemed to shake the ground.

'What do you bet,' Sykes said with a thin bitter face, 'that there were refugees aboard who didn't believe me?'

People were pouring across the ice now to the safer Kuban country of the south bank, but Red machine-guns were dropping scattered bursts among them and a few fell. On the other side, White Army artillery was wheeling into position to protect the crossing until the last military train was over.

As we moved off, I saw a stream of wounded from the hospital, some on crutches and sticks, some still wearing only pyjamas, some half-dressed or covered with a blanket, weaving and staggering down to the ice determined not to be left behind. I was trying to pick out Puddy when Tommy reappeared with a route to the Mission train. He took one look at the sick men and swung round to me.

'Where's Puddy?' he demanded, and when I told him what had happened at the hospital he immediately got permission from Sykes to make a last search among the staggering column of men.

The route to the yards was also under fire, with occasional scattered bursts of machine-gun bullets and an occasional shell, but the day was growing misty now and it was probably this that made our passage easy. As the grey haze came down, the Red machine-gun fire became haphazard because the men behind the weapons couldn't see what they were shooting at and we made it to the yards without harm. The refugees were as aware as we were what would happen to them if they didn't get across the river, and they were fighting for places on train roofs and buffers, even on the engines. Some were climbing on to the station buildings and trying to jump from there on to the trains. Those who made it invariably knocked off others.

More were jammed behind barriers, watched by police and railway officials with soldiers to back them up. The din was unbelievable and when the barriers broke under the pressure of several thousand frantic people, carriage doors were torn off in the mêlée and people were ejected like pips from an orange from the scramble, crushed or with broken limbs. Within seconds, they were fighting for places with the people already on trains and every single inch of every piece of rolling stock seemed to be covered with frantic people and surrounded by hundreds more using their fists and boots and suitcases and bundles to bludgeon their way aboard.

In the uproar, C Flight was broken up and we had to shout to the men to stick close together. They didn't need telling that if they became separated they might not make it, and somehow we thrust our way through the yelling crowd with fixed faces and unseeing eyes. Like the refugees, we knew that stopping to help others could probably only result in more deaths.

Tommy caught us up as we reached the Mission train. His face was tragic. 'He wasn't there,' he said.

I knew he was wondering how he could ever face Olga again, but there was nothing I could do to help him.

'I want to request permission to stay and find him,' he said.

My face felt like stone as I refused.

'We can't leave him!' he said.

I jerked a hand at the seething mob of refugees. There seemed to be millions of them now and they were all flowing towards the river from the town. To move back into them was impossible.

Sykes appeared and Tommy turned on him with his request. Sykes' expression seemed frozen.

'Tommy,' he said, and I knew he was feeling as much like an executioner as I did. 'We have all these men to get to safety and it's three hundred miles to the coast. We've lost Munro and Stagg and Jasper. You're needed here. I can't give you permission.'

Tommy stared at him for a moment as if he hated him, then he seemed to relax, aware of the hopelessness of a search. He managed a twisted smile. 'I guess you're right, sir,' he said. 'You must be.'

The train moved off as soon as we crammed ourselves aboard. As it began to jerk, there was a stampede by the refugees to climb on to the steps and running boards. At the other side of the river there was another colossal jam of trains and, as soon as we stopped, we climbed down, formed up and marched to another, longer train waiting a mile away on the southbound line.

There were a few empty cars for us, and officers and men of all regiments and all departments in South Russia were jammed in together – infantry, engineers, railway officers, artillerymen, RAF, Pay Corps. In the next fifteen hours we covered no more than five miles and we were still nearly two hundred from Ekaterinodar. Alongside the track the stream of people still trudged south. There were a few soldiers among them and once we saw a whole crowd of them outside a vodka factory, firing at barrels with their rifles and holding cups, mugs, tin cans, even their mouths under the spouting liquid.

A week later at Tikhoretskaya we found we'd left one scene of chaos for another. A few refugee trains still arrived, but with the army and the population contaminated by typhus, they were greeted with cries of 'Anybody who's alive get out'. Only a few haggard ghosts managed it.

The lines were blocked everywhere by abandoned rolling stock. Everyone seemed to be starving and desertions from the army were now numbering tens of thousands. Those who remained were limping and exhausted and useless as fighting men. Among them, tame as pet dogs, were abandoned horses, wandering about searching for non-existent fodder, and nibbling at wooden palisades in desperation.

From what we could gather, Novorossiisk was even worse. Down there, the last step for everybody before the sea, the refugees were arriving in hordes, half of them sick and all entirely without shelter in a town where there was no food and no fuel. The White armies had collapsed completely.

Sykes, who'd been to Mission Headquarters, returned with a grim face. 'Munro's safe,' he said. 'The train he was on was reported just north of Rostov days ago. He should be in Novorossiisk by now. Train 643 crossed, too, so they're safe as well. We were just in time ourselves, because Rostov's fallen.'

'What about Puddy?' Tommy asked.

Sykes' eyes glittered. 'When the Reds arrived,' he said, in a voice as dry as the rustle of winter leaves, 'they murdered the merchants and any White officers they found, and then drenched the hospital with petrol and set it on fire with what was left of the sick and wounded still inside.'

Tommy glanced at me then he turned away, his face sick-looking, and I couldn't find a single word to say to him.

Chapter 9

The Kuban countryside seemed more relentlessly cruel than ever in the icy grip of the snow, patches of trees standing out blackly against the whiteness and contrasting with the iron-grey sky.

We were cold and tired and it seemed weeks since we'd washed or changed our clothes. And we were hungry – especially Slingsby, who could never find enough to eat. 'Perhaps we'd better start eating each other,' he suggested, trying a joke to cheer us up. 'Tommy ought to taste pretty good with salt and pepper.'

He started to sing.

"If I had the wings of a Camel
ar, far away would I roam;
I'd fly to my friends in old England
And never no more come back home."

We needed a few light hearts like Slingsby's because all the time, to depress us further, there was that vast crowd of humanity streaming south alongside the railway track. Orders had gone out now from White headquarters that refugees were to be turned off all southbound trains which were to be taken over by the army, and the stream of people trudging down the banks of the frozen River Kuban looked like a crowd returning from a football final. Only this crowd was never-ending. It went on and on and on – as far as you could see in both directions, for ever, it seemed.

'Why didn't they stay where they were?' Tommy demanded. 'Surely they must have known that it's among the refugees that the Reds are looking for the aristocrats and merchants and White officers they hate so much. What's going to happen to them all?'

'A few are getting away to Constantinople and Prinkipo,' I said. 'A few have got to Shanghai and some even to Europe and America. As for the rest—' I shrugged, oppressed by a problem to which I couldn't see a solution '—only the troops and their dependants will get away.'

Tommy sighed. He seemed to have recovered a little from the news about Puddy. Puddy had been right all along. Though he'd dodged death on the occasion of his capture, it had only been because it was waiting elsewhere for a later meeting with him, and I knew what was in Tommy's mind because he'd settled down again to writing his vast letters to Olga.

'They'll never be able to come back to Russia,' he said. 'And this is their home. I know what I'd feel if I were told I could never go back to the States.

'I'd marry her if she'd let me,' he went on. 'Then she'd be safe because she'd be the wife of a British officer.'

'You in love with her, Tommy?' I asked.

He looked at me for a moment. 'I guess I have a very high regard for her,' he said stiffly. 'And there've been plenty of marriages of convenience lately – guys marrying girls to get 'em out of Russia. It doesn't mean a thing, I guess, but it does enable the girl to get a passport so she can reach safety. Now that there's no Puddy to take care of her, she'll maybe be glad to accept.'

–

Ekaterinodar had now become the White capital, but it could hardly be called efficient because every office where some struggling officer tried to bring order to the crumbling armies was inundated by wailing, protesting refugees, demanding protection, transport, food, shelter or even news of lost relatives. The wealthy were still there, still demanding preferential treatment and often getting it, but with the telephone exchange damaged, half the lines were out of order and little could be achieved because all communication was by men on horseback, in cars or on foot.

We found billets for ourselves in a big brick mansion that was already packed with officers from the British Mission who, like us, were being recalled to the coast. One of them was an artillery officer who was worried sick because two of his subalterns who'd been instructing Russian batteries had disappeared in the chaos and he had no idea how or where to look for them. The place was frozen up but we managed to build a fire with the remains of a shed in the garden and heated enough hot water to have a primitive bath and change our underclothes.

The news that fresh aeroplanes were waiting for us in Novorossiisk cheered us a little.

'Oh, joy,' Slingsby said. 'Just to get up out of this mess will be lovely!'

This time the aircraft were to be new ones, not worn-out has-beens from the Middle East and, like Slingsby, I began to look forward to the chance of getting into the air. Apart from times like these when events lurched into horror, I'd always derived enormous pleasure from being in the Air Force and found great beauty in the empty pastures of the sky.

I'd been living on the ground for so long in crowded filthy conditions a breath of clean wind on my face would have done me the world of good, and the thought of lifting a Camel off, going up a like a whirlwind with the engine pounding out its peculiar crackling roar in front of me, left me with faraway eyes. I was an airman and I wanted to be in the air, to see the fabric rippling in the slipstream, to smell the dope and the castor oil, and feel the joy of putting an aeroplane through its paces. It seemed such a time since I'd handled a machine I began to be afraid I might not be able to.

Slingsby seemed to sense what I was thinking. 'I've been worrying I'll have forgotten, *mon brave*,' he said. 'But it's like riding *une bicyclette*, isn't it? You never really forget, do you?'

'No,' I said. 'You never forget.'

As we came through the Caucasus, it was still bitterly cold and the land was shrouded with mist. There was an air of desolation and doom about Novorossiisk because, when the huge avalanche of refugees and wrecked regiments had descended on it, it had become nothing but a huge camp of starving people, terrifying the local inhabitants. During the long retreat, over two hundred thousand men, women and children had died of typhus, smallpox, starvation or exposure, whole trainloads of them including the crews. Now all the hordes of desperate survivors had poured into Novorossiisk, stumbling and weak and too disheartened to make any attempt to protect themselves; bodies seemed to be everywhere, and the hospitals were besieged by sick, frozen, hungry people for whom nothing could be done because the drugs had all long since disappeared, so that they simply crept into any corner they could find and waited either to die or recover. One officer lay for a fortnight in a cupboard before recovering.

The typhus was reaping a dreadful harvest and people who'd once lived in palatial homes were reduced to squalid cellars without even the simplest sanitary arrangements. Despair seemed to be the one emotion in the city, because they all knew that when the British disappeared there would be nothing to protect them from Budenny's cavalry.

Looking for Munro, I found myself outside one of the embarkation offices. It was being run by a British major.

'We took over because the Russians were taking bribes,' he said. 'And they never learn. The ones who were privileged in the old days still expect privilege.' He gestured at the crowds outside. '*With all this!*'

He'd heard nothing of Munro but he said there was a British-controlled hospital on the edge of the town and that they'd already started getting the sick and wounded on to the ships. Tommy went to the Red Cross vessel alongside the wharf while I went to the hospital. It was in a big house outside the city and was a little better than the Russian hospitals I'd seen, but not a great deal, because even here they were overworked and in a hurry.

'Have you seen how many men we've got here?' the doctor in charge said. 'They've come from all over South Russia, and by all means. Some have come on hospital trains, some have come on Mission trains, some have been brought in by their own men, some have been brought in by Russians, some have even been brought in by German and Austrian ex-prisoners of war. Some came in on their own two feet. Some of them could speak. Some of them couldn't because they were unconscious. Some were in full uniform with all their papers and pay books. Some were in their shirts or wrapped in a blanket because their hospital train had stalled and they'd been transferred, and all their belongings and paybooks were lost.'

'The chap I'm looking for's a short chap,' I said. 'With a big bony nose. And he's got scars all over his face from a crash and, because he'd had two broken legs, he walks with a bad limp.'

The doctor gave a tired smile. 'After four years of war in Europe,' he pointed out, 'there are a lot of men with damaged legs and scarred faces.'

'You couldn't miss him,' I pleaded. 'He was that sort of chap. His accent was so thick you might even think he was a Pole or an Armenian, and he wasn't noted for his good temper either.' A thought struck me. 'Have you a piano?'

He nodded. 'There's one in the ballroom. We used to give concerts to the sick when there was time.'

'Didn't you ever have anyone who tried to play it? This chap would.'

He thought for a moment. 'Come to think of it,' he said, 'there *was* one officer. And he did use a stick. Look, can you come back tomorrow? I'll get the padre on to it.'

Tommy's face was grim when I met him. 'Nothing doing,' he said. 'I tried everything. An accent like a Seminole Indian's, his sticks, his carved-up face – even the way he played the piano.'

I managed a faint smile. 'I thought of all those, too.'

Tommy was depressed because he'd spent the whole morning on the waterfront among the refugees and he'd hated every moment of it. With an American's warm-hearted wish to help others less well off than himself, it had shredded his nerves and his temper and none of his inquiries had produced any sign of Olga.

'She's bound to be all right, though,' I said. 'We know her train got here and Abramov was an intelligent man. He'd see she was safe.'

He frowned, far from convinced. 'I wish we could start flying again,' he said. 'The Whites are supposed to be moving into the Crimea and they could hold out there against anything the Reds send against them. We could do a lot of good there.'

Several of the Camels had been unloaded and stood in a square of barbed wire without their wings, and we stared at them longingly.

'Look good, don't they?' Tommy said. 'First time I took one up I was terrified. In the end I decided it was the best machine they ever built.'

He'd heard a rumour that they were fitting out a new train for us in the yards but I didn't believe it because the only way we could go in a train was north and I knew Sykes had long since been to the Crimea looking for somewhere we could touch down near the submarine base at Balaclava.

'Didn't your lot once get involved in something there?' Tommy asked.

I nodded. 'Yes. It was another disaster. I don't think Russia suits us.'

The next day, as we were setting off again to look for Munro, we heard the news of the White evacuation of Odessa. The western flank of Denikin's army had made its way there but had left the town too quickly so that civilians had fought with one another for the few ships and boats that were left. They'd killed one another, committed suicide and drowned themselves in the docks and, as the Reds had swept in, the criminals among them had emerged from their holes to murder and steal.

Tommy's face was bleak. 'That's what's going to happen here when *we* go,' he said.

We searched the ships once more and this time I went with Tommy because he begged me to.

'I can't fight 'em off any more,' he said. 'I gave away every bit of money I had on me.'

The staffs of the hospital ships had done their work carefully and there were half a dozen unconscious men they thought might answer to Munro's description. Since they had no idea of the men's identities, we were asked to go aboard and see if we knew them. But none of them was Munro and we left feeling depressed and miserable and got a lift in an ambulance to the hospital. They appeared to be evacuating patients.

The doctor explained. 'We've heard we're pulling out altogether,' he said. 'Lloyd George and Clemenceau think the anti-Bolshevik cause here's lost.'

'And those two half-wits have done as much as anybody to lose it,' I said.

He shrugged and shunted me to the padre, a tall willowy man with a pale saintly face. He gave me a queer look as I told him why I was there.

'Ah, yes,' he said, in the sort of plummy voice that sounds well from a pulpit. 'I think we've found your Captain Munro.'

'Where is he?'

He reached into a drawer and fished out a handkerchief tied at the corners. As he opened it in silence, I recognized Munro's watch and chain and letters addressed to him in Barbara Hatherley's writing. I knew exactly what it meant.

'What happened?' I asked.

'The man who played on our piano wasn't your Captain Munro,' the padre said. 'That was a mistake. It was another man. We found these on a man who'd been wounded when his hospital train was attacked by Green Guards near Rostov. They belonged to a man who'd died of typhus. He was asked to hand them in for despatch to the next of kin. Would you care to return them?'

I wanted to weep. 'Four years in France,' I said. 'Right from the beginning. He survived every kind of catastrophe it was possible to survive, and then he has to die in some rotten Russian hospital gasping his life out with a disease given to him by a flea.'

The priest sighed. 'It's God's will, my son.'

It seemed to me a strange way of manifesting it and I said so.

The padre frowned. 'God works in a mysterious way,' he insisted.

He pushed the handkerchief towards me and I picked it up without a word, not knowing what to say, or even what to think, or even if I were capable of thought. Munro had always been an awkward cuss but he'd saved my life more than once and I just couldn't bear to think of him dead.

'I just hope they've got a piano in heaven,' I said.

I couldn't imagine how I was going to break the news to Barbara Hatherley but, when I got back to the billet, I tried. It was a job I'd always hated doing, and I'd become an expert at setting down sympathetic words while managing to shut out all thoughts of the man I wrote about. Munro was different, though, and I finished the letter with difficulty. At the same time I wrote to his parents and to Charley who'd served as a nurse in France with Munro's girl. She'd get in touch somehow and she had a great gift of understanding.

I'd just thrown down the pen and sealed the letters for the post when I heard a commotion outside. 'You can't come in here,' the padre's high voice was saying. 'This place is reserved for British officers.'

'Nevertheless I come,' a voice said firmly in reply. 'I am British pilot. I look for Major Martin Falconer, of Royal Air Force.'

Tommy, who was reading a magazine opposite me, looked up and our eyes met, then we both dropped what we were doing and dived for the door. We reached it together, jamming the entrance, and fighting our way through, fetched up panting in the hall. There, by the outer door, leaning on a stick, one leg swathed in bandages and splints, was Puddy.

He was pale and gaunt but he was grinning all over his handsome face and the stick went flying as he hobbled forward. As he reached us, he stumbled and almost fell, but we caught him and, pushing a pompous major of artillery out of a chair without so much as a by-your-leave, we lowered him into it.

'How in God's name did you get here?' I asked.

'I walk,' he said.

'All the way?'

'Most of the way. Sometimes I ride a little, but mostly I walk. Was difficult.'

'But—' Tommy wore a shamefaced look '—we heard—'

Puddy nodded sadly. 'That they burn the hospital? Is true, this. Everybody in it. But I am not there. I am left.'

Tommy was obviously suffering from a guilt complex. 'I wanted to stay behind to find you,' he said.

Puddy grinned. 'Is good job you didn't,' he said. 'After your train leave very few get away. But me – I have leave already. I cross the ice in the dark that night.'

'But your ankle?' I said. 'Is it still broken?'

'Oh, yes.' Puddy shrugged. 'Is still broken. But only a little bit now.'

–

There was nothing to celebrate with but a little army rum, but we made do with that. Anybody with the courage to make his way from Rostov to Novorossiisk – even 'riding a little' – with a broken ankle deserved toasting and Puddy was regarded with something akin to awe by the other officers.

'Is surprising,' he said, 'how much you do when you must.' He smiled. 'Soon, I find Olga. Train Number 643 is in the town. Tomorrow I find out where I go to fetch her. I have uncle who is business chap in Paris. Has been there many years. We go there together when this is all over.' He looked sad. 'And I think now it is over very soon.' Then his smile returned. 'And what about Officer Jock? How is he? Playing the piano somewhere, I think.'

I drew a deep breath. I still had the letters to Munro's parents and Barbara Hatherley and Charley in my pocket. 'I've just been writing to his home,' I said. 'He died of *tif*.'

Puddy's jaw dropped. 'Is not possible,' he said. 'Officer Jock has lived after much disaster. Simply is not possible.'

'I've got his belongings in my pocket,' I said. 'They found them on the body. He's dead.'

Chapter 10

But he wasn't. Incredibly, he wasn't!

Three days later he turned up in a car from British Mission Headquarters. Like Puddy he was pale and weak, with cracked lips and discoloured teeth, and had lost about a stone in weight. Because they'd shaved his head on the hospital train, he also looked like someone just out of a prison camp but he was alive and in high spirits because his adventures since we'd last seen him had been extraordinary.

'When they got me aboard yon fast train south,' he said, 'Ah decided Ah liked it fine because the feller in the next bunk was yon Rhatanyi an' we were able tae have a wee crack aboot flyin'.'

'But why in heaven's name weren't you here waiting for us then?' I asked.

Munro was obviously enjoying his story. 'Because Ah've only just arrived,' he said.

'Mahkno's boys derailed us near Makayevka. There was a lot o' shootin' an' it seemed best tae lie low for a wee whiley. When it was all over, Ah went tae find ma belongin's but the car I'd been in was a wreck an' Rhatanyi had disappeared. Ah managed tae get on anither train but the engine ran dry an' Ah thought Ah was aboot tae dee when – mon, ye'll never guess, yon feller on the horse, what was his name, Machikov, that Shkura feller who rescued us in the mist when we were stuck oot on the steppes – damned if he didnae happen along.'

'I don't believe it!'

'Aye, it's true.' Munro's voice rose half a dozen octaves. 'He recognized me, mon! Me! Hector Munro! They'd found the wreck of the train I'd been on and fished oot a few sick and wounded but a lot had died since. They had some sledge things wi' a few survivors in 'em so they stuck me in one wi' a wee laddie who'd lost a leg in the wreck. At the end o' the week, Ah was better enough for 'em tae tie me tae a saddle.'

'And you made your way into Rostov?' Tommy asked.

'Na, mon!' Munro sounded contemptuous. 'Yon Machikov had ideas that were a gey sight better than that. We went north to Starocherkassk and crossed the Don near there – wi' the Reds only five miles away forbye. The ice was so thick they built fires to show the way across an' we spent the night in a village on the ither side, the whole lot o' us curled roond each ither tae keep warm. The next day the snow was so thick the ponies sank up tae their knees an' Ah had a fringe o' icicles all roond ma cap, jangling taegether like the crystals on a chandelier. Talk aboot "She shall have music wherever she goes". Ah sounded like a set o' empty wine glasses on a tray held by a waiter wi' the shakes.'

We got hold of some more rum and started celebrating all over again. We'd been luckier than we'd ever expected and come out of the campaign virtually unharmed.

'Ah feel like a wee tune,' Munro said. 'Is there a piano in the place?'

Slingsby found it, as the doctor had said, in what had once been the ballroom. It was without a back but Munro was unperturbed.

'It'll mebbe play better wi'oot,' he said.

In five minutes every man in the place – even the pompous artilleryman – was standing round him singing. One of the other officers – a Scots Guardsman no less! – proved to be an expert on a mouth organ, and another man had his banjo with him, and it developed into quite a party. There wasn't much to drink and we were chiefly intoxicated by our own noise, but considering what was outside in Novorossiisk we had a lot to be thankful for.

'Is wonderful,' Puddy crowed. 'We are all together again. All we want now is for Olga.'

–

We were just about to set off in search of her the following day when Sykes turned up with orders that no one, officer or man, was to leave billets.

'There's something on,' he said. 'Orders from Mission HQ. I've to report there.'

Puddy looked worried when I told everybody what was happening.

'I must to find Olga,' he said.

'And I'm coming with you,' Tommy said.

'Orders are that *no one's* to leave,' I said. 'Puddy can get away with it. He's Russian.'

'And I'm American,' Tommy pointed out. 'So they can't shoot me or hang me because it would create an international incident. I shan't be in the RAF much longer, anyway, because when I get away from here, I'm going home and King George and all his ministers won't stop me.'

'All right,' I said. 'I think I can cover for you. But don't waste time. If it's evacuation they might march us on to a ship straight away.'

British Mission Headquarters had been set up in a block of offices belonging to a cement works at the other side of the town and the artillery had positioned guns to protect it in case the Reds burst through the defences, or the Whites, who were beginning to regard us as traitors, tried to rush the place. I could hear the firing to the north as I waited for Sykes to return.

Blanketing snow began to fall and the streets looked black and icy as he appeared. His face was grim.

'Fall the men in, Brat,' he said. 'We're going back.'

'Back? Where to?'

'Ekat. Holman was at HQ. He'd got everybody in. Staff, tank officers, gunners, me. Every regiment in the British Army. It seems Ekat's been aban-doned prematurely and what's left of the British

Mission there's reported that there are several thousand women and children still in the city and the surrounding countryside. They're the families of White soldiers and if the Reds arrive before we can get reinforcements up there, every one of 'em's going to die.'

He paused and cleared his throat. 'Holman's given his word that we shan't leave till they're all evacuated to Novorossiisk. He's gone against orders to do it and because of that he can't order anybody to go. We've to ask for volunteers to get 'em out.'

When we went outside the riggers and fitters and all the ancillary tradesmen and soldiers attached to the squadron were drawn up in a hollow square. Sykes didn't waste time on preliminaries but, putting the case to them straight away, asked volunteers to take one pace forward. For a moment there was a long aching silence then, with a crunch of feet, every single man moved. I was thinking of the bare cold countryside between Ekat and Novorossiisk and the chances that in the end we might have to walk the whole distance back through the bitter cold with the Reds and Mahkno's Greens hanging on the fringes of the column. It wasn't a thought that cheered me up but for the life of me I couldn't have refused that step forward.

Sykes drew a deep breath and I could see he was pleased with the reaction.

'Thank you,' he said. 'I'm very proud.' He turned to me. 'Every man to have his rifle and full equipment,' he ordered. 'Together with rations for three days. Find out if there are any sick and leave them behind to guard the baggage.'

Tommy had appeared when I returned to the billet but there was no sign of Puddy.

'The train wasn't there,' Tommy said. 'So I thought I'd better get back. Puddy commandeered a horse and set off to find it. He's got a revolver and all his pockets are full of ammunition. He might not be able to walk, but he sure knows how to take care of himself and Olga. The train's just outside the town. What's on?'

'We're going back to Ekat,' I said.

His jaw dropped. 'What!' he gasped. 'I don't believe it!'

'You'd better start,' I said. 'We leave at once.'

—

It took a week to evacuate the stranded families, and their gratitude was pitiable to see. They'd all thought they were going to die and when British troops turned up eager to help them, they simply dissolved into tears. Carts and sledges were rounded up and those who couldn't be crammed into trains were sent south by road with an armed escort of British soldiers.

With Slingsby, an engineer officer, a languid but highly efficient young man from the Household Cavalry and a mixed group of air mechanics and soldiers, I found myself manning a truck in an armoured train guarding the line, while Tommy was on horseback scouring the countryside outside Ekat with Russian cavalry, shepherding in the women and children. Holman had always had tremendous authority with the Russians and now he was everywhere at once. Among the White families there were a few who had no call on our support, but they all got it.

A few of the trains were attacked by Greens who tried to block the track with logs and stones. Our chief concern was to stop them clambering aboard or blowing up the track or the cars that contained our precious ammunition. Some of the raiding bands were Reds and some were Greens and some were even mixed, and when the engine pulling the armoured train broke down I found myself stationed with Slingsby at a halt halfway to Novorossiisk where we fortified the station buildings in case the Greens tried to cut the line there. Though there were a few shots and Slingsby did his best to provoke an incident just for sheer devilment, nothing happened to worry us and, as the last train came through with Sykes and the others on board, we clambered up the steps to join them.

When we reached Novorossiisk, it was obvious that the place was on its last legs. The harbour looked empty now and there were only a few transports left, though there were a great many more battleships in the bay, most of them British, their guns trained on the passes through the Caucasus above the town.

'It looks like the end o' the world,' Munro said.

Novorossiisk was a sick, terrified city. It was freezingly cold still, with the grey-black sea stark against the icy whiteness of the land and the Bora, the high wind of the coast, piercing the clothes of the starving scarecrows crowding into whatever shelter they could find. Ships were covered with ice and the gale swept through the pitiful shelters that had been thrown up, and blew down the camps of the Kalmuk soldiers above the town. Every now and then the place shook to the salvos of the warships in the bay – the British *Empress of India* and the French *Waldeck-Rousseau* – which were flinging shells towards the north where the Red cavalry were approaching, the concussion thudding across the town, beating against the ears and rattling the windows.

Tommy was worried. 'There's no sign of Puddy,' he said.

'Perhaps he got himself and Olga on to one of the other ships,' I pointed out. 'It's possible. Perhaps, even, they've separated and she's got away with Abramov and the others.'

On the docks Ordnance Corps men were stripping the breech blocks from field guns, and destroying ammunition, supplies and equipment. As we went to look for our aeroplanes, there seemed to be even more bodies than before, sprawled in doorways and alleyways and in the gutter where it was as easy to fall over them as it was to slip on the ice.

The evacuation was getting out of hand now and the mobs of refugees kept massing outside the evacuation office where a squad of Guardsmen with fixed bayonets had been stationed. With the civilian shipping lines cancelling their calls at Russian ports, the only way to safety was aboard a barge, a launch, a tug or on a British transport or man-of-war, and people were being murdered for the little money they possessed, so that enough could be gathered to bribe some Levantine tramp skipper. Even the loyal Whites were mutinying against Denikin now and demanding that Wrangel should be given the command. In return, Denikin was said to have cashiered him and several members of his staff and was demanding his departure from Russian terri- tory. With orders not to interfere the British were keeping well out of it.

The next day it was announced that no civilians were to be allowed on military transports unless they were part of a White officer's family, and large numbers of Kuban Cossacks immediately began to make their way on foot along the coast towards Turkey. The guns of the *Empress of India* were still playing on the approaches to the city but the Reds had already managed to infiltrate the defences and had released all the prisoners from the city jail, who were beginning to prey on the refugees as they huddled in everything they possessed, surrounded by candles, ikons and holy pictures to which they clung even when they'd had to give up their warm clothing. They jammed every hotel, and huge warehouses smelling of coal and rats were full of more homeless exhausted people dying of privation, while every train took away a fresh load of sick who'd been picked up in the streets. The peninsula seemed to be full of the dying debris of White regiments and was the nearest thing to purgatory you could wish to see, because there was now nowhere else to flee to and hope had ended.

–

I don't know how we got through the next days. Munro pounded the piano like a lunatic but, with all that horror outside, it was hard work trying to cheer us up. It was like a great weight on your shoulders that you knew you couldn't shift because there was nothing – not one thing – any of us could do to improve matters. Whatever else the Bolsheviks got out it all, they would inherit such misery it would be years before it was forgotten.

Fortunately there was a batch of letters waiting for me from Charley – all out of date but the last we'd receive. 'You'd never believe it,' she wrote, 'but we're all going to Mexico!!!! Father's been offered a job with some petroleum company in Vera Cruz. I don't think he's going to get paid very much but he's broke, anyway, and it seems too good an opportunity to miss, because all passages are paid. And as it seems it'll be years before you come home, I'm going, too.'

Oh, charming, I thought. Charming! Just when I was looking forward to seeing her again, she was disappearing into the blue.

The next morning we destroyed our aeroplanes. Flight-Sergeant Merry was on the verge of tears and there wasn't a man whose face wasn't fixed and bleak. We'd continued to hope against hope that some miracle would let us fly them across the narrow strip of sea to the Crimea, and the mechanics had been hanging around them for days, doing a little adjusting here and there for the moment when they could really get to work. Now we lifted them from the flat cars and pulled them one after the other through the screaming wind to the docks where a waiting Mark IV tank rumbled over them, crushing them into a tangle of wood, fabric, wire and metal.

When we'd destroyed the Camels, we started on brand-new DH9s still in their crates and when the tank driver had finished, he set his controls and throttle and climbed out as the machine began to lumber for the wharfside. A great sheet of black water lifted into the air as it disappeared over the side.

There was no longer a future for us in Russia and we were wishing it could be over. Tommy was still watching anxiously for some sign of Puddy, but he still didn't turn up. The *Empress of India's* guns went on booming out, shaking the town with their roar, but the situation was clearly hopeless because the Whites no longer had any confidence in Denikin and were considering only how to save themselves.

A few of us were asked if we were prepared to go to the Crimea and Flight-Sergeant Merry appeared indignantly to say he'd been offered a commission in the White Army if he'd stay and fight on.

'I'd look fine, wouldn't I, sir?' he said. 'Shot in the back like all the rest before I knew where I was.'

None of us was very enthusiastic about fighting on in a dying cause that the British government didn't support and which didn't concern us, anyway, and the thing fell through. Then on 27 March orders for evacuation came through. Denikin and his staff were already aboard a French destroyer and only a few volunteers were holding the passes north of the town against the Reds. Sidorin had been asked to hold the foothills with his Don Cossacks but he'd refused and headed instead for Georgia.

By this time we were billeted in an empty warehouse near the docks, officers and men all together. It was cold and cheerless but at least the Bora had stopped blowing. The following day we marched to the harbour.

Winches were whining and the rusty sheaves of hoists creaked as baggage and kit were hoisted aboard. Clattering donkey engines filled the cold air with steam and the warships began to flash signals to each other in preparation for departure. During the afternoon a tremendous explosion rocked the town as the petrol tanks were blown up, and the dense smoke began to blow across the harbour on the high wind.

Bolshevik troopers were in the northern outskirts of the town now and the refugees were growing frantic, so that heavy guards had been posted on the ships' gangways to prevent them being rushed. They were camped along the wharves in thousands, sitting on their belongings and building bonfires, the whole foreshore packed with people and animals – whole families on their knees praying for help.

The place was completely demoralized and we all knew that the Reds and Greens were only waiting for the British to leave before they swept through the town. They were in all the high buildings and on the bluffs, sniping and watching everything that happened. Then, as we waited to file aboard, a man on a shaggy starving pony came hurtling into sight, to rein the animal in so hard it slithered and fell. Scrambling to his feet, he started to shout – 'The Bolsheviks are coming! The Bolsheviks are coming!' – and almost immediately, over the rising din of panicking people I heard a rushing sound like an express train hurtling through the air.

There was a crash and a fountain of water rose in the harbour as the first Bolshevik shell arrived, and immediately the mob of refugees began to surge to every point where they thought there might be shelter. Amid the horses, camels and waggons that thronged the shore, they pleaded with the Black Sea shipmasters, knowing that the only alternative was death. Distraught fathers began to offer us money to marry their daughters, and every kind of horror and bribery was perpetrated for the one thing they all wanted and couldn't get – a passage to safety.

Everywhere I looked there were hurrying waggons, perambulators and hand carts as people tried to get their belongings to the ships. Some were old couples with all their worldly possessions, some merchants wheeling the last contents of their shops in the hope of starting up again somewhere else. White troops began to throw away the shoulder straps that indicated their regiments and officers tore off their epaulettes because the Reds had an obsession about them and liked to nail them to their owner's shoulders if he was captured.

As I watched a businessman offering whole suit-cases of useless White roubles in exchange for a passage, there was a commotion further along the quay. A shot rang out and I saw the body of a woman who'd committed suicide being carried away by her relatives. Another shell arrived, and one or two people dived into the icy water to swim out to anchored ships and clutch nets and trailing ropes to haul themselves on board. They were merely dried off and set ashore again so that no one could have any doubts that even that way was closed to them.

The shelling stopped and the wailing, screaming people rushed back to the quays, a solid mass covering the shore, the piers, the mole and the breakwater, pleading, begging, cursing the British for leaving them. A group of Kuban Cossacks waiting in a group round their striped flag, watched silently, exhausted men on jaded horses, all that remained after six years of fighting of the forty thousand who'd first left home for the wars. The only things they possessed were their horses, their clothes, their weapons and that fluttering symbol of their independence.

Not one of the men of C Flight had moved. Nearby, White cavalrymen were boarding a French steamer. Then the signal was given and we marched to the gangway of the Greek ship that was to take us off, pushing through crowds of Kalmuks and refugees who grabbed for our hands to kiss them, even at our clothes. We could do nothing but brush them away and say we were sorry. Just behind us an American steamer, which had arrived the day before with munitions, had also joined in the evacuation and had started to cram people aboard, demanding no tickets and asking no questions, its crew prepared out of sheer decency to do what they could to alleviate some of the horror.

The oily water between the ship and the quayside was full of trunks, clothes, furniture, even bodies. I was swept up the gangplank under the eye of a platoon of Guardsmen and found myself on the deck, gazing back at the land from a deck jammed with men, almost the last to embark. Tommy was staring across the wharves. 'I hope Puddy and Olga are all right,' he kept saying.

Near the French ship, the cavalrymen were shooting their horses rather than have them fall into the hands of the Reds. Several who had no more ammunition had even pushed them into the sea and the animals were swimming around, neighing in terror. I felt sick and weary, and hated everybody, especially the politicians responsible for this appalling tragedy we were living through.

The French ship went astern from the wharf, the screw pounding. The dusk was falling and one after the other more ships began to leave the quays. The

Greek transport began to tremble as the engines were started and sailors started to haul in the gangplank. It was almost free of the wharf when I saw Puddy coming through the crowd, riding an exhausted horse.

'There's Puddy,' I yelled.

'He's alone,' Tommy said. 'Olga must be on one of the other ships!'

As Puddy slipped from the animal's back and began to hobble forward, pushing people aside in his efforts to reach us, we stopped the hauling in of the gangway and began to yell.

'Come on, Puddy! Hurry, for God's sake!'

He was only fifty yards away when the Bolshevik gun opened up again. The express-train noise filled my ears, then another shell landed in the bay. Immediately the crowds alongside the ship seemed to heave and scatter and I saw a swirl of terrified people running for cover brush against the struggling lonely figure fighting its way towards us. As he fell, Tommy yelled, then Slingsby – inevitably Slingsby – his pale anonymous face alight with the prospect of excitement, scrambled over the rail and made a tremendous leap for the shore. He almost didn't make it but he managed to scramble to the quay and started running to Puddy. I immediately started pushing towards the gangway, Tommy right behind me.

As we fought our way ashore, another shell landed in the bay, a great deal nearer this time, and the Greek sailors started to panic. The next one burst on the edge of the wharf where the French ship had been and I saw splinters of concrete and wood fly into the air. The screams of the crowd as they scattered came like the howl of banshees and every ship in the harbour started to move. Men began to run and the guards scrambled aboard as ropes were cast off.

Sykes and Munro and several others were struggling with the Greeks by the gangplank, trying to stop the ship moving, but no one was taking any notice and the ship started to back off, with the officers yelling from the bridge and the gangway hanging over the side, trailing its ropes in the water.

'The American ship, Brat,' Sykes yelled. 'Get aboard the American ship!'

A Russian soldier in the rags of a uniform tried to grab me but I pushed him aside and kept on running. Out of the corner of my eye I saw the Greek ship drawing further away, then I lost it as I plunged into that half-crazed mass of frantic people, barging through them and shoving them aside, aware of Tommy alongside me, plucking figures from our path with his great hands.

I thought we'd never reach Puddy but we managed it at last. He was down on one knee, his stick lost under the feet of the crowd, and he lifted his head and managed a bleak thin smile as we hauled him upright, a hand under each arm, and began to rush him along the quay while Slingsby stood behind us, half-crouched, a revolver in his fist, defying the lot of them to rush him. No one did.

The American ship was full of White soldiers and refugees and they were just hauling in their gangplank as we fell in a heap on the deck. Almost immediately, I saw the land begin to recede.

The *Empress of India* and the *Waldeck-Rousseau* were still firing over the town, and I could hear the wailing of the refugees who'd been left behind coming across the water. There was nothing now to stop Budenny's cavalry sweeping into Novorossiisk and butchering the lot of them.

An officer in a blue uniform appeared alongside me. 'Where in tarnation do you think you're going?' he shouted.

Tommy looked up. 'You American?'

'Yeah.' The officer gestured. 'And we don't stop before we reach the States.'

Slingsby's cherubic face split in a beaming smile. 'Leave in New York,' he yelled.

I looked at Tommy. 'Charley's on that side of the Atlantic,' I said.

'And I'll not need to resign my commission. I'll just stay home where I belong. Oh boy!'

Then we became aware of Puddy dragging himself to his feet. His face was grey and thin and dangerous-looking.

'Where's Olga?' Tommy asked. 'What ship's she on?'

Puddy moved along the deck, refusing to say anything, and Tommy pushed after him, loudly demanding to know what had happened, and little by little, it all came out. He'd found what was left of Train Number 643 on a sidings outside the city, sealed to the track where it had been abandoned by the frozen rust-coloured stalactites from its own waste pipes. The engine and most of the coaches had gone and all that was left was one Pullman coach containing the bodies of two dozen *tif* victims, Dr Abramov, and three of the nurses.

'But not Olga!' Tommy yelled. 'For God's sake, Puddy! Not Olga!'

Puddy's head nodded. 'Yes,' he said. 'Olga. I saw her myself.'

—

In the growing darkness I watched the land drawing away. Fires were breaking out all over the city and I could see lines of blazing torches approaching the quayside and hear the crackle of rifle fire. I didn't know what to think. Russia had attracted me with its vastness, and I knew that a lifetime later I'd still have nostalgic feelings about the place. But at that moment I felt ice-cold and as if tears were falling on my heart, one after the other, in a slow monotonous rhythm that seemed impossible to bear.

Tommy was standing nearby, his arm round Puddy's shoulders in a gesture that was desperately sad in its suggestion of friendship and suffering. He was staring at the shore with empty eyes and I knew what he was thinking. His wounds were grievous and they were not physical but spiritual, and his soul was crying out for a miracle that would never happen.

He was bewildered. He'd been more than prepared to give his life and it hadn't worked out that way. He'd survived and, in spite of everything, Puddy had survived, too. Munro had survived, Sykes had survived, Slingsby had survived, I'd survived. By all the odds of war, any one of us could have died because we were soldiers and death was part of a soldier's pay. But we'd all come through sound in wind and limb and it had been Olga who'd gone into the darkness, shy, gentle, pretty, soulful, romantic little Olga, for whom Tommy had fallen, dying alone in a Pullman carriage full of dead men and women, untended, uncared for, unnoticed. I just couldn't understand it and it drove every other thought from my mind – England, the knowledge that we were leaving, Charley, everything.

I couldn't watch the land any more and I turned away, close to tears. The American officer who was supervising the stowing of the gangway was watching me with concern in his expression. 'Y'all right, son?' he asked.

I nodded and drew a deep breath, so deep it hurt my chest. 'Yes,' I said. 'I'm all right. I've just grown old suddenly, that's all.'